A FRIEND CALLED ENOCH

THE CALLED
BOOK 6

KENNETH A. WINTER

WildernessLessons

JOIN MY READERS' GROUP FOR UPDATES AND FUTURE RELEASES

Please join my Readers' Group so i can send you a free book, as well as updates and information about future releases, etc.

See the back of the book for details on how to sign up.

~

A Friend Called Enoch

"The Called" – Book 6 (a series of novellas)

Published by:

Kenneth A. Winter

WildernessLessons, LLC

Richmond, Virginia

United States of America

kenwinter.org

wildernesslessons.com

Edited by Sheryl Martin Hash

Cover design by Scott Campbell Design

ISBN 978-1-9568660-8-7 (soft cover)

ISBN 978-1-9568660-9-4 (e-book)

ISBN 978-1-9568661-0-0 (large print)

Library of Congress Control Number: 2022914670

References to *The Book of Enoch* are taken from *The Book of Enoch*, The Apocrypha and Pseudepigrapha of the Old Testament, edited by H. R. Charles Oxford, published by The Clarendon Press

DEDICATION

In memory of
all those who came before us
and faithfully walked with God

∾

… He was known as a person who pleased God.
And it is impossible to please God without faith.
(Hebrews 11:5-6)

∾

CONTENTS

FROM THE AUTHOR

A word of explanation for those of you who are new to my writing.

You will notice that whenever i use the pronoun "I" referring to myself, i have chosen to use a lowercase "i." This only applies to me personally (in the Preface). i do not impose my personal conviction on any of the characters in this book. It is not a typographical error. i know this is contrary to proper English grammar and accepted editorial style guides. i drive editors (and "spell check") crazy by doing this. But years ago, the Lord convicted me – personally – that in all things i must decrease and He must increase.

And as a way of continuing personal reminder, from that day forward, i have chosen to use a lowercase "i" whenever referring to myself. Because of the same conviction, i use a capital letter for any pronoun referring to God throughout the entire book. The style guide for the New Living Translation (NLT) does not share that conviction. However, you will see that i have intentionally made that slight revision and capitalized any pronoun referring to God in my quotations of Scripture from the NLT. If i have violated any style guides as a result, please accept my apology, but i must honor this conviction.

Lastly, regarding this matter – this is a <u>personal</u> conviction – and i share it only so you will understand why i have chosen to deviate from normal editorial practice. i am in no way suggesting or endeavoring to have anyone else subscribe to my conviction. Thanks for your understanding.

PREFACE

~

This fictional novella is the sixth book in the series titled, *The Called*, which is about ordinary people God called to use in extraordinary ways. As i've said before, we tend to elevate the people we read about in Scripture and place them on a pedestal far beyond our reach. We then tend to think, "Of course God used them. They had extraordinary strength or extraordinary faith. But God could never use an ordinary person like me."

But nothing could be further from the truth. The reality is that throughout history God has used the ordinary to accomplish the extraordinary – and He has empowered them through His Holy Spirit.

Enoch was one of those people. Once i started telling people that i planned to write this novella, i have been delighted to hear how many people have been impacted by his story in the Bible. Some have told me how they were challenged to walk with God through his testimony as it is recorded in Scripture. And to be completely transparent, his story is a part of my testimony as well. Lives are still being impacted today by a man who lived over 5,000 years ago!

What makes that even more interesting is that we are told very little about him. He is referenced in only four passages in Scripture: Genesis 5:18-24, Luke 3:37, Hebrews 11:5-6, and Jude 14-15. He is the seventh of the ten antediluvian (pre-flood) patriarchs from Adam to Noah, noted more as a postscript between the stories of Adam and Noah.

Based upon the time frames set forth in Genesis 5, we know that his life overlapped with the lives of all the antediluvian patriarchs, except his great grandson, Noah, who was born after Enoch was gone. It is safe to presume that Enoch would have interacted with his grandfather, Mahalalel; his father, Jared; his son, Methuselah; and his grandson, Lamech. But the Bible does not tell us whether or not he had a close relationship with his older ancestors.

Bear in mind that God had told Adam and Eve to be fruitful and multiply. They did not have a small family. Jewish tradition teaches they had fifty-six sons and quite probably an equal number of daughters. (i think i just heard all the women reading this take a great sigh in empathy for Eve!)

Their children (except Abel) would have many children themselves . . . and so on. Thus, by the time Enoch came on the scene, the extended family would have been in the hundreds of thousands, and possibly in the millions – and growing. So again, we don't know if Adam and Enoch ever actually knew one another. At the very least the stories about Adam would have been passed down through the generations. For the purpose of this story, i have chosen to write it in a way that Enoch and Adam did know one another, and they enjoyed a close relationship.

Also, in Genesis 5 we read: *"Now Enoch lived sixty-five years, and fathered Methuselah.* **Then** *Enoch walked with God three hundred years after he fathered Methuselah. . . ."* i have emboldened the word "then," because i take the word literally. i do not believe Enoch was walking with God prior to the birth of Methuselah. Rather, i believe something occurred in his life at the time of his son's birth that caused him to repent and turn – and begin to walk with God. Accordingly, you will see that belief reflected in the story.

Along those lines, there is also a question as to the words "Enoch walked with God." Did they literally walk with one another, or is it a figurative term referencing his close relationship with God? i believe it is both, so you will see that belief reflected in the story as well.

Lastly, i think we often miss the fact that Enoch was a prophet. Jude, the half-brother of Jesus, writes in his epistle that Enoch was in fact a prophet of God. i think that is an important point as we look at his life and also the circumstances surrounding the fact that *"God took him."*[3] There are only two men who ever lived who did not die – Enoch and Elijah.[4] Both of them were prophets, and some speculate (myself included) that those men may be the two witnesses who return in the last days as recorded in Revelation 11.

In the Book of Hebrews we read, *"It is destined for people to die once, and after this comes judgment."*[5] The fact that neither Enoch nor Elijah has yet experienced death seems to qualify them for the job of the two witnesses, who will be killed when their assignment is completed. You will see a reference in the story to this possibility.

Lastly, you will find i use references to "The Book of Enoch"[6] in the story. The Book of Enoch is an apocryphal book, which means its authenticity is in question. It is most definitely not a part of the canon of Scripture. But Jude actually quotes from the book in his epistle. So at least those two verses[7] must be considered as being inspired by God. The apostle Peter also appears to have used a portion of those writings as background for his epistles, 1 Peter and 2 Peter. i do not advocate that "The Book of Enoch" is anything beyond an apocryphal work, but i did determine that a portion of its writings that clearly align with Scripture needed to be included as a part of this story.

i have taken great care to include more background information in this preface than i have in my other books, because i want you to clearly see the line between the factual elements of this story and the portions that are plausible fiction. My desire is that you are introduced to Enoch the person and not merely as a postscript. He was an ordinary man God used – and is still using – in extraordinary ways!

So, i invite you to sit back and enjoy this walk through the life of Enoch and the other characters i believe are an important part of his story. You will recognize many names in the story from the first few chapters of the Book of Genesis. As in all my books, i have added background details about them that are not in Scripture so we might see them as people and not just names.

i have also added completely fictional characters to round out the narrative. They often represent people we know existed but are never provided details about, such as parents, spouses, or children. Included in the back of this book is a character listing to clarify the historical vs. fictional elements of each character.

Whenever i directly quote Scripture during the story, it is italicized. The Scripture references are also included as an appendix in the book. The remaining instances of dialogue related to individuals from Scripture that are not italicized are a part of the fictional story that helps advance the narrative.

One of my greatest joys as a Bible teacher and author is when readers tell me they were prompted to go to the Bible and read the biblical account after reading one of my books; i hope you will do so as well. None of my books is intended to be a substitute for God's Word – rather, i hope they will lead you to spend time in His Word.

Finally, as i have already indicated, my prayer is you will see Enoch through fresh eyes – and be challenged to live out *your* walk with the Lord with the same boldness, humility, and courage he displayed. And most importantly, i pray you will be challenged to be an "ordinary" follower with the willingness and faith to be used by God in extraordinary ways that will impact not only this generation, but also the generations to come . . . until our Lord returns!

1

A SIGHT TO BEHOLD

∽

I've been living with Methuselah since my wife, Dayana, passed away. He is a good son and has been a blessing to me from the Lord God Jehovah since the day he was born. His wife, Mira, has been more than patient and gracious with me. I am a terrible house guest; my daughter-in-law never knows whether I will be joining them for meals, which makes food preparations difficult. Truth be told, I have probably been absent from the dinner table more often than I have been there – but she has never once complained.

My schedule fluctuates because I often leave our home to go on long walks. I never know where the walks will lead or how long I will be gone. Those details are all in the hands of the One with whom I walk.

Today began like most every other day. I joined the men who sit at the gates of our village. Just as I have done many times throughout the past 300 years, I declared the words the Lord had spoken to me just the day before:

"The Holy Great One will come forth from His dwelling, and He will tread upon the earth, even on Mount Sinai. He will appear from His camp and appear in the strength of His might from the heaven of heavens.

All will be smitten with fear. The watchers will quake, and great fear and trembling will seize them unto the ends of the earth.

The high mountains will be shaken. The high hills will be made low, and will melt like wax before the flame. The earth will be wholly rent in sunder, and all that is upon the earth will perish.

And there will be a judgment upon all. But with the righteous He will make peace. He will protect the elect, and His mercy will be upon them. They will all belong to God. They will be prospered, and they will all be blessed. He will help them all, and light will appear unto them. He will make peace with them.

And behold! He cometh with ten thousands of His holy ones to execute judgment upon all – to destroy all the ungodly, and to convict all flesh of all the works of their ungodliness which they have committed, and of all the hard things they have spoken against Him."[1]

But just like the many times before, instead of remorse and repentance, the response to those words was silence. Those who sat before me acted as if they were deaf and dumb. There was no sorrow over sin. There was no fear of judgment. There was no fear of the Holy Great One!

We live in a day when wickedness prevails. All of creation has seemingly turned away from its Creator, and turned toward all manner and practice of evil. Jehovah God has called upon me to be His prophet, proclaiming His words of coming judgment to this evil generation.

But each day I have found that hearts have become more hardened against the words of the Lord. Each day I become more aware that members of my family are the only remaining righteous ones on the earth – but that is not even true of all of my family.

For some time now, Jehovah God has permitted me to walk with Him. On most occasions I do not see Him in the way you see me. His presence beside me is most often not in physical form – but in many ways, it is even more palpable.

He speaks with me, and I speak with Him. He has invited me to walk with Him in a way similar to how He once walked with the patriarch Adam before the great fall. He tells me what is on His heart, and I tell Him what is on mine. He tells me things that are just for me – and He tells me things that I am to tell others.

We walk and talk for hours. Sometimes we walk to places that are near and familiar. But at other times, He takes me to places that are far away from here – to breathtaking sights that have not yet been corrupted by evil and still display all the pure beauty of His creation.

He once took me to the pinnacle of a mountain range, overlooking what appeared to be an entire region of the earth. As I stood there, I marveled at the Creator's handiwork and His majesty.

As I did so, He said, "Enoch, this is but a glimpse. Your view here is limited. But one day, when you are in My dwelling place, your vision will be unhindered. You will be able to see My creation from My perspective. All that is now dim will be made bright. All that is now unclear will be brought into focus. In the meantime, you and I will continue our walks, because there is so much more I want you to see and do."

That brings me back to today. He and I have walked together for many years and today He took me to a place unlike any other I have ever seen. It is a large city filled with buildings that look very different from those I have seen before. And it is inhabited by people who look very different from me. I know it is a special place, but initially I could not have told you why.

But I am getting ahead of myself in telling my story, so allow me to go back and tell you what transpired leading up to this day. And by the way, if later in your travels you happen to encounter my daughter-in-law, Mira, please convey my apologies for having missed another one of her delicious meals!

~

2

THE SON OF JARED

～

$\mathscr{I}$ am the seventh generation of my family to walk on this earth. It's hard to believe, but every one of my direct ancestors was still living when I was born:

Adam was 622 years old.
His son, Seth, was 492 years old.
His son, Enosh, was 387 years old.
His son, Kenan, was 297 years old.
His son, my grandfather, Mahalalel, was 227 years old.
His son, my father, Jared, was 162 years old.

As you can imagine, I am not my parents' eldest son. Given my father's age at the time of my birth, I am well down the list of children in the order of our birth. Several of my oldest brothers were already grandfathers by the time I was born – making me a great uncle to a multitude of children older than I was.

I had a host of siblings, cousins, uncles, and aunts beyond what anyone could count. The Creator had told Adam and Eve, "*Be fruitful and multiply and fill the earth.*"[1] And they had done so! Everyone could trace our ancestral line back to them, but from there the family tree sprouted more branches than a banyan tree. By the time I was born, Adam's descendants had formed countless tribes and peoples living in an equally countless number of villages, cities, and regions. Some said his descendants numbered in the millions.

Though we all shared one common ancestor, we had become a very diverse people, practicing all forms of ungodliness as we each pursued evil desires. We no longer acknowledged Jehovah as our God and Creator; rather, we had become worshipers of different aspects of His creation. Some worshiped the sun and the heavens. Others worshiped the animals of the earth, the fish of the sea, or the birds of the air. Some elevated the lusts of the flesh and declared their godless practices were a form of worship. In seven generations, we had strayed as far away from our Creator as we possibly could. That was true of my father, his father, and most of Seth's descendants.

My father, like the generations before him, was a farmer. My grandfather, Mahalalel, settled his family on an expanse of land along the Tigris River we now call home. He staked out a section of land he deemed to be more fertile than the rest. My father and his many brothers did as well. The land was free to whomever claimed it. But because of the curse of sin, farming – even on this fertile ground – came at great cost.

Jehovah God had told Adam after he and Eve sinned, *"I have placed a curse on the ground. All your life you will struggle to scratch a living from it. It will grow thorns and thistles for you, though you will eat of its grains. All your life you will sweat to produce food . . . until your dying day."*[2] Adam's descendants were now feeling the sting of that curse.

Many of our people turned away from the Creator because of that punishment. They completely lost sight that the Creator was not responsible for the curse; rather, it was the result of Adam and Eve's sin. Our people ignored the fact that a holy and righteous God cannot overlook sin.

To the consternation of our patriarchs, Adam and Seth, my immediate family attributes whatever success we enjoy from the land to the river god. Twice each year, our family presents an offering of the first fruits of the harvest to the river god in thanksgiving – for the plentiful bounty provided and as an act of supplication for continued blessings. My father once told me, "The God of Adam rejected the first fruits offering presented by our ancestor Cain, but the river god has never once been so discourteous." This caused me to grow up with a strong resentment for the Lord God Jehovah.

When I was ten years old, Adam and Eve came to live in our village. Though most of the villagers acted and believed very differently from them, Adam and Eve were still respected as honored ancestors and were warmly welcomed into the village.

I hadn't yet fully comprehended who they were; I just knew they were old. As a matter of fact, they were the most ancient people I had ever seen! I knew we were somehow related, but it was still too confusing for me to understand. My parents instructed me to call them "Abot" and "Matre" out of respect for their position in our family as patriarch and matriarch – though I didn't really understand what those titles meant either.

They situated their home near ours, so I saw them often. My parents frequently invited them to have a meal with us. Abot would always tell me stories about the ancient days. He was joyful as he shared some of the tales, but other stories made him sad.

Though most of his accounts were from long ago, he made it seem like they happened yesterday. I had never heard anyone speak of the Creator with such affection. It was as if the Creator was his dearest friend – a friend he had betrayed.

The more time I spent with Abot and Matre, the more I was drawn to them. My relationship with my grandfather, Mahalalel, and my great-grandfather, Kenan, had never been close. But I wanted to be around Abot and Matre continually so I could hear more of their stories.

One day Abot asked me, "Enoch, do you know why Matre and I came to your village?"

When I shook my head, he replied, "Because the Creator wanted me to tell you these stories. He wants you to know about Him . . . and even more importantly, He wants you to know Him!"

～

3

THE VERY BEGINNING

~

*A*bot began to tell me his personal story. "Unlike you, Enoch, I have no childhood memories. I never needed to learn how to walk, how to talk, or how to care for myself like you did. I had no parents to teach me like you do. The Lord God Creator formed my body from dust and, like everything else He created, He did so perfectly.

"I had no blemish, no defect, and no deficiency," Abot continued. "The Creator didn't have to experiment by creating earlier versions of me until He found the one that best suited His plan. He had me in mind before He created time itself.

"But the true miracle of my creation is not that He created me from the dust of the earth. The true miracle is that I am the product of His breath. He breathed into my nostrils – filling my mind, my will, my emotions, and my spirit with His likeness. Unlike any of His other creations, He created me in His image and gave me charge and dominion over all His other creations.

"My first memory is the moment I opened my eyes and took in my first breath. There I was, face to face with my Creator. Enoch, imagine if you can, what it was like to enter the world – not through your mother's womb – but as a fully grown man with the capacity to think, feel, and communicate as an adult from the moment of your first breath," Abot told me.

"From that moment, I was able to speak to God, and I was able to understand Him when He spoke to me. And I am mindful that the Creator gave me that gift of language, first and foremost, so I could communicate with Him. Yes, I would later use language to talk with others, just like you do, but primarily He intended I use that gift to speak with Him – in praise, in worship, and in fellowship. That was a truth I would soon fail to consider.

"On the first day of my life, God planted a magnificent garden filled with all sorts of beautiful trees, many of which produced delicious fruit. Many of those trees and bushes you have here in your garden. But there is an important difference – it was a perfect place, without any thorns or thistles. He told me to tend to it and care for it. Never before had there been such a garden, and never before had there been anyone to look after it. The One who created the garden instructed me how to nurture it – perfectly and lovingly – in the same way He had created it.

"But then He added this warning: '*You may freely eat any fruit in the garden except fruit from the tree of the knowledge of good and evil* in the center of the garden. *If you eat of its fruit, you will surely die.*'[1]

"He showed concern for His garden, but He showed even greater concern for me. He said, '*It is not good for the man to be alone. I will make a companion who will help him.*'[2] He proceeded to form every kind of animal and bird from the dust, just as He had created me. But He did not breathe into their nostrils. Rather, He simply spoke a word and each one awakened. He placed them before me and told me to choose an appropriate name for each one. But first, He gave me a name – Adam – meaning 'son of the earth.' Since He had created me from dust, it was certainly fitting!

"As the birds and animals passed before me," Abot continued, "I observed there were two of every kind – male and female. Each one had a companion, but I realized there was no companion for me. But I knew the Creator had not made an oversight. Nothing catches Him by surprise! He had always known I would need a companion of my own kind. In His wisdom, though, He wanted me to come to that same conclusion. He did not want me to take my companion for granted, but rather recognize my need and know He specifically created her for me.

"The Lord God directed me to lie down, and I immediately fell asleep. It was the first time I had ever slept – and it was a deep sleep. The Creator opened my side and removed one of my ribs, using it to create the woman He also patterned in His own image. Then He closed up my side, leaving a faint scar.

"See, Enoch, the scar is right here," Abot said, opening his cloak.

"It's not a blemish; rather, it's a reminder for Matre and me that she was bone of my bone and flesh of my flesh. I did not experience any pain or discomfort during or after the Creator's surgery. I awoke feeling rested and fully restored.

"As soon as my eyes fell upon Matre, I was overwhelmed by her beauty and gentleness. I exclaimed, '*At last! She is part of my own flesh and bone! She will be called "woman," because she was taken out of a man.*'[3]

"The Lord God Creator blessed us both saying, '*Multiply and fill the earth and subdue it. Be masters over the fish and birds and all the animals. I have given you the seed-bearing plants throughout the earth, and all the fruit trees for your food. And I have given all the grasses and other green plants to the animals and birds for their food.*'"[4]

～

4

WE WALKED WITH HIM . . .

~

*a*bot continued with his story. "As that first day came to an end, God looked over all He had created and announced it was excellent in every way. He had labored six days to create the light and the darkness, the earth and the waters, food for us and the animals, work for us to do, and the gift of companionship with each other. He declared the seventh day would be a day of rest.

"But even more than that, He had granted us fellowship with Him. Our Creator made us with the desire to have a close relationship with Him, and He desired to have fellowship with His creation. He proclaimed the seventh day would be set aside for rest and a special day of fellowship with Him. He declared it to be holy.

"During those early days, the Lord God would come walk in the garden with Matre and me in the coolness of the evening. He walked with us and talked with us and reminded us we were His creation, and He was our Creator. He was the only parent we would ever have. He never tired of our questions, patiently answering each one. We looked forward to those walks, and I believe He did as well!

"Matre and I never grew weary of laboring in the garden. Our fellowship with God gave our lives purpose, and our work gave us meaning. Our walks with God enabled us to know Him more and know each other more intimately. Words will never adequately describe what our lives were like in those early days.

"But one day, everything changed. Matre and I were tending to different areas of the garden when she was approached by the serpent. He was the most beautiful of all creatures. I had marveled at his beauty and cleverness the day he was created. He was one of the few animals given the ability to speak, and on previous days Matre and I were delighted when he would talk with us.

"But on this day, the serpent was different. He was under the control of another being – one called Lucifer. Matre did not know the serpent was under Lucifer's influence. Nonetheless, we both knew the words being spoken by the serpent were contrary to God's commands.

"'*Did God really say you must not eat any of the fruit in the garden?*'[(1)] the serpent asked Matre.

"She replied, '*Of course we may eat it. It's only the fruit from the tree at the center of the garden that we are not allowed to eat. God says we must not eat it or even touch it, or we will die.*'[(2)]

"'You won't die!' the serpent hissed. '*God knows that your eyes will be opened when you eat it. You will become just like God, knowing everything, both good and evil.*'[(3)]

"Enoch, I need you to understand that Matre knew what the serpent was telling her was contrary to God's command. She knew God had told us not to eat from the tree under any circumstances. But the fruit looked inviting. And now the serpent was telling her it would make her wise. At that moment, the creation decided she knew better than her Creator.

"And so did I, because when Eve extended the fruit to me to eat, I also knew it was contradictory to God's command. The moment we took a bite, a sense of shame washed over us both. We suddenly became aware that we were naked, and we reached out for leaves and branches to cover ourselves.

"We knew what we had done was wrong. We had never before experienced feelings of guilt and shame. And when we later heard the Creator approaching, we hid from Him. Until that moment, we had never considered hiding from Him. We had always run to Him!

"I heard the Lord call out, '*Adam, where are you?*'[4]

"As He approached the spot where I was hiding, I replied, '*I heard you, so I hid. I was afraid because I was naked.*'[5]

"'*Who told you that you were naked?*' the Creator asked. '*Have you eaten the fruit I commanded you not to eat?*'[6]

"'*Yes,*' I replied with my eyes averted from the Creator, '*but it was the woman You gave me who brought me the fruit, and I ate it.*'[7]

"I was sorry as soon as I uttered those words. I was blaming Matre – my companion, my wife, and my helpmate. How could I even consider shifting the responsibility to her? She had not made me disobey God; I had made that decision on my own.

"And what's more, the Creator had charged me with the responsibility of tending to the garden – not her. And He had specifically told me not to eat the fruit of that tree. If anything, I should have kept her from doing so. But instead, I had disregarded the Creator and done what was right in my own eyes. Who was I to blame Matre for my disobedience? I now felt even more ashamed!

"The Creator turned to Matre and asked, '*How could you do such a thing?*'[8]

"Then she did the same thing I tried – she passed the blame off to someone else! '*The serpent tricked me!*' she replied. '*That's why I ate it.*'"[9]

Just then my mother called out, "Enoch, it is time for you to go to bed!"

5

. . . UNTIL WE COULD NO MORE

$\sim$

I couldn't wait to find Abot the next morning so I could hear the rest of his story. As soon as I saw him, I asked, "What happened? What did the Creator do?"

He told me to come sit beside him. Once I was settled, he continued. "The Lord God Creator turned to the serpent and said, '*Because you have done this, you are cursed more than all animals, domestic and wild. You will crawl on your belly, groveling in the dust as long as you live. And I will cause hostility between you and the woman, and between your offspring and her offspring. He will strike your head, and you will strike His heel.*'[(1)]

"Immediately, the serpent's legs disappeared, and he began to slither in the dirt. He opened his mouth to speak but the only sound he could make was a hiss. An animal that had been the most beautiful had become the most despised. He quickly slithered away into the shadows.

"God turned to Matre and said, '*I will sharpen the pain of your pregnancy, and in pain you will give birth. And you will desire to control your husband, but he will rule over you.'"* [2]

"So is that why my mother cried out in pain when she gave birth to my little sister?" I asked.

"Yes, it is," Abot replied, then continued. "The Creator then turned to me and said, '*Since you listened to your wife and ate from the tree whose fruit I commanded you not to eat, the ground is cursed because of you. All your life you will struggle to scratch a living from it. It will grow thorns and thistles for you, though you will eat of its grains. By the sweat of your brow will you have food to eat until you return to the ground from which you were made. For you were made from dust, and to dust you will return.'* [3]

"The Creator then called out for two beautiful animals grazing nearby to come to Him. They looked lovingly into the eyes of their Creator who told them He would require they sacrifice their lives so Matre and I could be clothed in their skins. Both animals responded by saying, 'Whatever You require of us, we will do. Because we know that You love us and will only do what is best for us!'

"With that, they laid down their lives, and death entered into this world. The Creator clothed Matre and me in their skins. I wept as I wrapped their skins around us, knowing that our sin had cost those beautiful creatures their lives, and that species would no longer exist because of their sacrifice for our sin. But that was only the beginning. I had not yet fully grasped the breadth of the consequence of our sin.

"My attention was turned back to the Creator when I heard Him say, '*Adam and Eve have become like Us, knowing both good and evil. What if they reach out, take fruit from the tree of life, and eat it? Then they will live forever!*' [4]

"I knew the Creator wasn't asking me; rather, He was speaking aloud to Himself. And I had come to realize that whenever He spoke about

Himself, He often used a plural pronoun. He had explained during one of our walks that there was more to Him than I could see. He said He was one God in three persons – Father, Son, and Holy Spirit. But I must confess that at the time, I couldn't quite comprehend what He was saying. And Enoch, I'm not so sure I completely understand it today.

"What I do know is the Lord banished Matre and me from the garden that day. He stationed His angels at the gates guarding the entrance. We would never be permitted to return. As the years passed, we found we could no longer remember where the garden was.

"We were exiled from the garden because of the tree of life. That tree was also located in the center of the garden but, unlike the tree of the knowledge of good and evil, we had been permitted by God to eat its fruit. But now that would no longer be the case. A consequence of our sin was that we – together with the animals and all those who came after us – would die a physical death. Our physical bodies would no longer live eternally. Death, disease, and decay would now be as much a part of our lives as birth. Everything had changed because of our disobedience!

"We eventually made our way to another parcel of land, which became our new home. We lived there until we came here. I cultivated it as the Creator had taught me, but it never even approached the beauty, splendor, or bounty of the garden. It provided us with some food, but we soon realized we needed to supplement our diets with meat – which meant that more animals and birds would need to die for our sakes. They were now all reproducing more of their kind, and their number was increasing.

"Not long after, Matre came to me with the news she was pregnant. It was time for *our* seed to grow in number! Matre had many questions about childbirth, and we both had more questions than ideas about raising a child. Without question that task would be greater than any other the Creator had placed before us to do. But, by His grace, He assured us He would be there to guide us along each step. And He was."

It was time for me to join the others and go work in the fields. As I left, Abot said, "I will continue my story the next time we are together."

6

THE SINS OF THE FATHER . . .

~

*M*y brother, Shep, was born one year after I was. With such a large family and such a wide age disparity between siblings, we usually had closer relationships with brothers and sisters nearest our age. Shep and I enjoyed the closest bond while growing up.

We enjoyed exploring the land. When we were young, we had fewer responsibilities than our older brothers. That gave us more time to explore the hills and the valley, as well as enjoy an afternoon swim in the river – a practice that continued even as we got older.

Though Abot often told me the beauty of the land paled in comparison to Eden, I still marveled at its magnificence. Even as a boy, I believed that a Master Creator had formed each delicate flower, each majestic tree, and each rolling hill. I was particularly in awe of the vibrancy and breadth of colors, each one as rich and brilliant as the other. I found myself wondering what everything would have looked like without all those spectacular colors – but I was thankful that would never be a concern.

My father taught us to thank the river god for all the beauty. But the more I listened to Abot, the more I began to think my father might be wrong. However, I decided I would continue to keep an open mind and listen to them both. Several weeks passed before Abot was able to continue with his story.

"Our firstborn son was also the first baby to *ever* be born," he told me. "Matre had seen many of the female animals in the garden give birth, but she had never seen another woman do so – nor was there another woman to ask. At the time of our son's birth, he was only the third human on the face of the earth.

"His birth was not without its pain and travail. After the birth, Matre informed me, 'God told me I would bear children with intense pain and suffering, but until I experienced it, I did not fully understand just how difficult it would be. But the Lord God Creator did not abandon me in my hour of need; with His *help, I brought forth a man!*'[(1)]

"We named him Cain, and for the first year of his life, he was our only child. His 'firsts' as a child were our 'firsts' as parents. His first steps were a victory for us. We learned there would be times he would fall down, but it would all be a part of his learning how to walk on his own. The Creator told us it was an important lesson for us – and him – to learn.

"Next came his first words. We watched as he struggled to learn to speak. Having never had that struggle ourselves, we could not completely under-stand. We had expected him to be able to speak from the moment he was born – just as we had done. But we quickly realized we needed to patiently teach and encourage him.

"Cain was almost one year old when our daughter, Awan, was born. Matre again experienced the pain and difficulty of childbirth, but this time she had a better idea of what to expect. It wasn't long before Cain considered himself his baby sister's protector. They were close, like you and Shep, from the very beginning. But that wasn't true of his feelings toward our next child, Abel.

"Cain was almost two when Abel was born. Even at that age, I could see a change in Cain. His attitude toward his baby brother was different from when Awan was born – maybe because he was younger then, but more than likely because Awan was a girl. Up until then, Cain had been my only son. But almost from the moment Abel was born, Cain saw him as a rival who inserted himself into the exclusive relationship Cain had enjoyed with me.

"I did everything I could to assure Cain of my love and the special place he would always hold as my firstborn son. Still, as he grew older, I observed his tendency to posture himself in a more favorable light than his brother. For example, I was blessed he wanted to learn everything I could teach him about being a good farmer, but I also knew part of his motivation was to be better at it than Abel.

"As time passed, Matre gave birth to many more children. On three occasions, she gave birth to twins. As a result, our family was growing rapidly. By the time Cain was sixteen, we had nineteen children. But it grieved me as a father that Cain continued to feel the need to compete with his brother. Gratefully, I never saw any sense of competition from Abel. Rather, he desired to have a close relationship with his older brother.

"As Abel got older, he chose to become a shepherd. I believe it grew out of his love for animals and his ability to care for them. But I also believe Cain's penchant for turning everything into a competition may have played into it. Though Abel never said, I wondered if he became a shepherd so his brother would not feel the need to compete as farmers.

"I was proud of both my sons in the way they went about their work. One day when Abel was fourteen years old, I remember telling him, 'Abel, you remind me of our Lord God Creator. You care for your flock, just as He cares for us. You protect each one, and when they stray, you seek them out.

You do not leave them or abandon them. I am proud of you for the choice you have made and for the way you attend to your duties.'

"Abel received my words humbly, but I saw Cain out of the corner of my eye as he scurried away. Apparently, he had heard what I told Abel."

7

. . . AND THE INIQUITY OF THE SON

~

*a*s I thought about Cain and Abel, it made me reflect on my relationship with Shep. I'm grateful that I never felt like he and I were in competition for our father's approval. Of course, I wasn't the eldest son. Perhaps that would have caused me to think differently. However, I don't believe so.

I saw the sadness in Abot's eyes as he continued with his story. "Later I told him, 'Cain, I am proud of both of you! My pride for one does not diminish my pride for the other. Don't resent what I have said to your brother. I have told you many times about how proud I am of you!'

"But sadly, Cain's resentment for Abel did not diminish. The sin nature that now dwelled within all of us fostered a selfish ambition in Cain that only increased. Nothing Matre and I did made any difference.

"When Cain was eighteen, Matre and I sat down with him and Awan and told them it was time for them to become united as husband and wife. The Lord God Creator had instructed us that when our sons came of age, they were to leave us and be joined to a woman. Awan and Cain had been close all their lives, and they had always known this day would come. They would now be the first of their brothers and sisters to marry. They were now the center of attention – which Cain relished.

"Over the years, Matre and I had become skilled in making clothing from the skins and hair of animals for our family to wear. Awan and two of her sisters had also developed that skill. We all worked together to make the most beautiful clothing we could for Awan and Cain to wear for their marriage celebration. The Creator Himself officiated over the exchange of vows.

"The events surrounding the marriage distracted Cain from his resentment toward his brother – at least for a little while. A short time later, the Creator told me the time had come for us to present a harvest offering to Him as an expression of our thanksgiving for His provision. I instructed Cain and Abel to gather the offering, and I reminded them that this was not a competition. 'Bring the best,' I said, 'because the Creator is worthy of the best!'

"Cain immediately set out collecting the best of the firstfruits of this year's harvest, but it was obvious he did see this as a competition with his brother. When the day for the presentation arrived, he proudly paraded his offering before God. He had enlisted several of his younger brothers and sisters to help him carry it all. The quality of the fruits and vegetables was quite impressive. When Cain bowed his head before the Creator, I watched him glance up to make sure God looked pleased with what he had brought.

"The Creator told him to stand to the side so Abel could present his offering. Abel walked in leading several of his spotless lambs. I think I saw Cain chuckle when two of the lambs bleated disrespectfully as they were led before the Lord. Cain obviously thought Abel's offering was inferior. Abel tied the lambs to a branch and bowed his head without a word.

"Everything was silent as God seemed to evaluate the two offerings. Suddenly, He spoke to my younger son: 'Abel, the day your father and mother sinned in the Garden of Eden, I slew two beautiful animals so the nakedness of your parents could be covered. The blood of those precious animals was shed so your parents' sin could be covered. Their blood was the true gift … a sacrifice … given by those two spotless animals.

"'Today, you have brought these unblemished lambs before Me from the best of your flock. You have presented them to me for their blood to be shed as an offering of thanksgiving to Me. You have sought nothing in return, just like these lambs, humbly and reverently presented to Me. Abel, I accept your offering of thanksgiving.'

"Then the Creator turned toward my older son and said, 'Cain, you are the firstborn son of Adam. You have all the rights and responsibilities that your position in birth entails. And yet, you have lived most of your life in the shadow of envy and resentment toward your brother. The serpent tempted your mother – and she in turn tempted your father – with the desire to have that which I had told them they could not have. They responded to that temptation with the same envy toward the fruit for what they thought it would bring, and resentment toward Me because I had told them they could not have it.

"'As a result, sin was birthed in their hearts and in this world. It is the same sin that dwells within your heart. That sin has tempted you to envy and resent your brother. It has led you to bring these fruits and vegetables before Me – not as an offering of thanksgiving – but as a means through which you hoped to validate your own selfish desires. You have come in the hope I will honor you above your brother.

"'Cain, I reject your offering because you have brought it to Me with iniquity in your heart. Turn from your wickedness and turn toward Me. Your enemy, the deceiver, lies in wait for you, just as he did your parents! Do not heed his voice!'"

～

8

WHY, BROTHER?

~

There were so many questions I wanted to ask Abot, but I decided to remain silent and let him continue with his story.

"I watched my son's horrified reaction to what the Creator said. I hoped he would be remorseful and repentant; but instead, he took the Creator's rebuke as another way Abel had bested him. He obviously blamed his brother for the reprimand he had received.

"The Lord God looked at Cain and asked, *'Why are you so angry? Why do you look so dejected? You will be accepted if you respond in the right way. But if you refuse to respond correctly, then watch out! Sin is waiting to attack and destroy you, and you must subdue it.'*[1]

"Cain abruptly turned and walked away, not even taking time to collect the offering he had brought God. He was embarrassed. His offering had been rejected, and he'd been rebuked in front of his family – including his younger brothers and sisters who looked up to him. I knew my son well enough to know he wasn't walking out in sorrow over his sin, he was seething with anger.

"I knew he wouldn't receive anything I said to him at that moment. I looked over at Awan, and she obviously thought the same. She knew when her husband got like this, no one could talk to him. And none of us had ever seen him this angry.

"I later learned what was going through Cain's mind after he stormed off. He apparently began to consider what his life would have been like if Abel had never been born. The more he thought about it, the better he liked it. Suddenly, a horrifying thought washed over him, and he began to warm to the idea.

"'Yes, that is the solution to my problem,' he thought. 'With Abel out of the way, everyone will pay me the honor and respect I am due. It will be as if he never existed.' At that moment, he heard a hissing sound from the corner of the room, he later told me, and then he saw something slither across the floor and out the door. Quickly, the tail of the serpent disappeared.

"Cain stayed by himself the rest of that day and night, but the next morning he rose early and set out to act on his plan. As he expected, Abel was already awake when he found him. His brother had always been the earlier riser. Cain approached him and said, 'Abel, I behaved badly yesterday before the Creator, our parents, and all of you. I was so surprised by what the Creator said I didn't know what to do. You've always understood Him better than I do. I wondered if you would be willing to help me make amends and do what I need to do.'

"'His ways are simple,' Abel responded, 'but sometimes they are difficult to live out. Not because of what He expects, but because of the pull within us to go our own way – just like Mother and Father did in the garden. They gave into that voice and did what they knew was wrong. And as a result, so do we. But the Creator is faithful to forgive us if we will repent of our ways and seek His forgiveness. That is what you must do, Cain. You must go to Him and repent and seek His forgiveness.'

"'I am the older brother,' Cain responded. 'I know these things – but sometimes I don't want to do what I know I am supposed to do. Will you go with me as I go to the Creator? Having you with me will give me the added courage I need to do what I must.'

"'It doesn't take courage, brother,' Abel replied. 'It takes a broken and contrite heart. But I will go with you if that is what you want.'

"'It would be a great encouragement to me,' Cain said. 'I saw the Creator heading toward the riverbank for an early morning walk when I was on my way to find you. We should be able to catch Him there if we hurry.'

"Cain began to lead the way, and Abel followed close behind. However, when the bushes formed a fork in the path, Cain went to the right. Abel quickly called out, 'No, brother, the riverbank is this way. We need to go to the left.'

"Abel made the correct turn, and Cain quickly made the adjustment to be right where he had always intended – following closely behind Abel. With the bushes surrounding them on both sides, and Abel's attention fixed on the path ahead, Cain removed the stone blade he was carrying at his waist. With one fluid motion, he reached around and held Abel's forehead with his left hand, and drew the blade across his brother's throat with his right.

"Abel's head fell back toward Cain's chest as his body collapsed. With his final breath, Abel looked up into Cain's eyes and mouthed, 'Why, brother?'"

Up until that point, Abot had been trying to maintain his composure as he told me what happened, but it became too much, and he began to weep.

"My precious son Abel was murdered at the hands of my firstborn son!" he cried out.

I knew there was nothing I could say or do that would console Abot. The grief and sorrow were as fresh at that moment as they had been all those many years before.

9

THE OUTCAST

~

$\mathcal{A}$ short time later, Abot was able to continue with his story. "As we later discovered, Cain buried Abel's body and covered his grave with underbrush, believing we would never find it.

"The sun was just beginning to rise higher in the sky as Cain returned to our homesite. We were now all awake and just beginning the workday. We were surprised to discover the Creator standing in the center of our camp. It was highly unusual for Him to join us at that time of day. As soon as He saw Cain, the Creator called out, '*Where is your brother? Where is Abel?*'[1]

"Cain knew the Creator knew all things, but still he attempted to deceive Him. He answered, '*I don't know! Am I supposed to keep track of him wherever he goes?*'[2]

"Just then Matre and I walked into the middle of the camp and stood beside the Creator. We could tell from His presence and His questions that something was wrong. We strained to hear Cain's answer.

"'*What have you done?*' the Lord demanded. '*Listen – your brother's blood cries out to Me from the ground. You have defiled the ground with your brother's blood. No longer will it yield abundant crops for you, no matter how hard you work. You are hereby banished from this place. From now on you will be a homeless fugitive on the earth, constantly wandering from place to place.*'"[3]

"It was as if the blade of a knife had been plunged into my heart as I struggled with the reality of God's words!" Abot exclaimed, as tears again formed in his eyes.

"'I am the firstborn son, my Lord,' Cain cried out. '*My punishment is too great for me to bear! You have banished me* from my world as I have known it and *from Your presence. You have made me a wandering fugitive. All who see me will try to kill me* . . . today and in the days to come!'[4]

"'*They will not kill you,*' the Lord replied, '*for I will give seven times your punishment to anyone who does.*'[5]

"The Lord then placed a mark on Cain's face as a warning to anyone who might try to kill him. One by one, all of our family turned our backs on him, the last being Matre and me. Our hearts were broken. We had lost two sons that day – as well as a daughter – as Awan followed her husband out of the camp.

"The journey of sin led them farther and farther away from us that day, as Cain and Awan made their way east. They did not know where they were going, but they knew they must place a considerable distance between themselves and us. Awan was expecting a child when they left our camp that day. She would soon give birth to our first grandson, whom they would name Enoch – just like you! When I look into your eyes, I often think of him – my first grandson whom, like the rest of Cain and Awan's children, I have never met.

"Awan had no one to help her when the time came to deliver the baby. Matre had been looking forward to helping her with the delivery because Awan had assisted her with the deliveries of many of our children.

"The journey of sin not only led them farther away from us in physical distance, but it also led them further away relationally from the Creator. Cain never repented of his sin; rather, he chose to grow in his wickedness, as did his offspring.

"Cain sired a multitude of children. Cain and Awan continued to have children until they were both well over 100 years old. Those sons and daughters were given to one another in marriage and each of them gave birth to large families. By the time Matre gave birth to our son – your patriarch, Seth – six generations had descended from Cain and Awan, with their extended family numbering in the tens of thousands. They were scattered throughout the land they called Nod.

"Each succeeding generation knew less and less about the Creator. By the time Cain's great-great-great-grandson, Lamech, was born, there was only a distant memory of God. Instead, the people chose to worship creation itself – the sun, the moon, the mountains, and the rivers. Also, they had no knowledge of Eden. There was, however, still some knowledge of Cain's murderous act, though none could recall the details or the fact he had killed his brother. The only memory was that a law had been established long ago – that anyone who kills Cain is to be punished seven times. But no one could tell you why.

"Lamech married two women, both of whom were his cousins. One was named Adah and the other was Zillah. Adah gave birth to a baby named Jabal, who later grew up to be a herdsman and was the first generation to live under a tent. She also gave birth to a second son, Jubal, and he became the first musician, inventing the harp and the flute.

"Enoch, now you know where the idea of living under tents began and where the harp and flute originated. Though I never saw Cain again, nor any of his offspring, this earth is still just a large village and what one person does can affect the entire village!

"Through Zillah, Lamech fathered Tubal-cain. He became the first forger of metal, producing instruments of bronze and iron. As a result, the crude weaponry we used gave way to the more advanced – swords and knives with metal blades, and spears and arrows with metal tips."

I interrupted. "Is that where we got the idea to make metal blades and tips for our knives and weapons, Abot?"

"Yes, it is," he replied. "Remember, we're just a large village. Even their beliefs have influenced the rest of our people. Your family's beliefs are no longer much different from the beliefs of Cain's descendants. Sadly, because of our sinful nature, we all have the proclivity to turn away from our Creator."

Then he continued with his story. "One day, Lamech used one of those knives to kill a young man who attacked and wounded him. No one knew the young man's motives. The only statement to the rest of the tribe was one uttered by Lamech himself with great arrogance – '*If anyone who kills Cain is to be punished seven times, anyone who takes revenge against me will be punished seventy-seven times.*'[6]

No one seemed to recall that it was God who had established the former – and no one seemed to care when Lamech boisterously exclaimed the latter."

∿

10

A PROMISED SAVIOR

~

It had been several weeks since I was able to sit with Abot and listen to his stories about our family history. It was harvest season for the wheat crop, and now that I was eleven, I was expected to do a greater share of the work in the fields.

One of the Creator's commands we still observed was resting on the seventh day of the week. In all honesty, I think it was less about being obedient to the Creator and more about our fathers realizing our bodies needed a day of rest.

I took advantage of one of those days to visit Abot in his tent. He picked right up with his story where he left off.

"I was 130 years of age when my son Seth was born, which meant over 120 years had passed between his birth and those of Cain, Awan, and Abel. With the large number of sons and daughters we welcomed into our family during those intervening years – as well as their succeeding generations – our extended family numbered well into the tens of thousands, just like Cain's.

"Though Matre gave birth to numerous sons between Abel and Seth, there was no mistaking that Seth was the one who looked most like me. The Creator told us Seth was a special gift from Him, which is why we named him Seth. His name means 'granted,' and as Matre said, 'God has granted me another son in place of Abel, the one Cain killed.'[1]

"I knew he was the son to whom I would pass along the birthright that normally belongs to the oldest son. Though the Creator occasionally visited us after Cain murdered Abel, those visits had ceased by the time Seth was born.

"We looked back on those days with sadness and regret – and we still do. Our disobedience has caused so much pain and suffering. Our hearts break when a mother or baby dies during childbirth, when a child is attacked by a wild animal, or when someone tragically dies as the result of an accident. We know each of those deaths is a consequence of our sin.

"We remember the days when the wolf grazed with the lamb, the leopard lay down with the calf, the hyena played with the antelope, and the lion ate straw like the ox. We remember how we labored without growing weary, and how the plants grew abundantly without the restrictions of weeds, thistles, or thorns. And how the garden was a place filled with joy.

"Though we had spent time face to face with the Creator, we did not know how to worship Him now that He was no longer visible. We had talked with Him many times, but we did not know how to speak with Him when we could not see Him. So, our relationship suffered. Our sin created distance from our Creator, and that separation left unrepaired created even more distance. We knew that better than anyone!

"The day we disobeyed and ate the forbidden fruit, the Creator said to the serpent, *'From now on, you and the woman will be enemies, and your offspring and her offspring will be enemies. He will crush your head, and you will strike His heel.'*[(2)]

"It was clear to Matre and me that one of our offspring would one day crush the head of the evil one. Though the serpent would strike at His heel, the fatal blow would one day come to the evil one. He would be destroyed and the world would be put back to the way it had been before the evil one tempted Matre and we disobeyed God."

"When Seth was slightly older than you are now, I told him what I am telling you, Enoch. His eyes lit up when he asked, 'Father, does that mean that even at the moment of your disobedience, the Creator already had the remedy for your sin in mind? Is it possible that hope is not lost? The Creator has promised to send a Savior – One who will crush the head of the evil one. He will crush sin itself. The evil one did not win. He lost. And in the Creator's perfect timing, all will be realized!'

"Seth continued on excitedly. 'Father, our Savior will come from your offspring. And He has given me hope that our Savior will come from my offspring. He is the ultimate birthright you have passed to me. He may come during our lifetimes, or He may come after we have returned to dust. But He will come! Father, there is great reason for us to have hope! And we must learn how to talk with the Creator and walk with Him, even when we can't see Him or hear His voice!'

"From that moment, Seth continued to walk righteously before God. He seized the promise the Creator had given and walked with Him by faith – and he still does today.

"When he came of age, we arranged for him to marry his niece, Chava, whose name means life. Her great-grandfather is one of Seth's older brothers. The Lord blessed Seth and Chava with many sons and daughters.

With each son, Seth asked the Lord God if this was the one who would crush the evil one, but each time the Creator told him, 'No.'

"However, when Seth was 105, Chava gave birth to a son they named Enosh. The night he was born, the Lord told me through a dream that the Savior would come through my grandson Enosh's offspring. When I awoke the following morning, I went straightaway to Seth's camp to tell him the news.

"None of us has any idea how long we will need to wait, but we rejoiced together in knowing we were one generation closer to His arrival! When Seth shared the news with Chava, she asked me if it would be appropriate to dedicate Enosh to the Lord in light of the tremendous honor the Lord was bestowing upon him.

"I realized that day, at the age of 235 years, I had never dedicated any of my children, grandchildren, or other descendants to the Lord. Though it was not a practice I had followed, I knew Chava was correct and it was something we needed to do – and I needed to be the one to dedicate him!"

≈

11

ONE CHILD IS DEDICATED, ANOTHER IS CONFUSED

～

"*E*noch, since I had never dedicated my children to the Lord, I wasn't quite sure what to do," Abot continued. "Seth, Chava, Matre, and I gathered, together with the child, along the riverbank the next morning.

"As the sun appeared over the horizon, I took Enosh in my arms and raised him toward the heavens. I called out, 'Lord God Creator, You are the Maker of all life. Every good gift we have comes from You – including this little one. You have created him and entrusted him to us, just as you have all my children, their children, and their children's children – those who are gathered here and those who are scattered about.

"'Create within this child a heart to walk with You and seek You in all things. Protect him from the evil one when he attempts to turn him away from You. As he grows, make Enosh into a mighty man who seeks You above all else and walks uprightly.

"'Grant him the wisdom, strength, and faith to lead the family You one day grant him, as well as all of us, to do the same. Raise up the Seed through him You will one day use to defeat the evil one, once and for all, according to Your promise. Protect that Seed and allow that we might see Him in our lifetime for the salvation and forgiveness of all.'"

Abot went on to tell me he had three great regrets in life. He regretted his sin in the garden – because all other regrets stemmed from his disobedience to God. He regretted his failure to raise Cain in the instruction and fear of the Lord as well as failing to recognize the errant path Cain had chosen. And he regretted he had not dedicated each of his children to the Lord. He wondered aloud if things would have been different in Cain's life – and in the lives of the generations following him – if he had done so.

But Abot's face brightened as he went on to tell me more about his grandson. "During Enosh's childhood, we began to hear about musical instruments, including the harp and the flute, being fashioned by the estranged members of our family. From the day these instruments were introduced to our camp, Enosh demonstrated a gift for playing them – creating beautiful melodies that soothed the soul and lifted the spirit. It wasn't long before everyone in camp was either humming or whistling the melodies Enosh played.

"My grandson was only a few years older than you are now when he came to me with an idea. 'Grandfather,' he began, 'we all know every good and perfect gift we have has come from the Creator. I believe that is true of the melodies I play on the flute and harp. I believe He has given them to us so we might present them back to Him as a verbal offering. Those melodies, together with the words we might add, become an expression of our praise and worship to the Lord God Creator.

"'Grandfather, you have often told me about your walks with the Creator in the garden. You have told me about the closeness you felt to God during those days. That is how I feel when I play my melodies to Him and lift up my voice to Him. I can't see Him physically, but I can see Him in my mind's eye, and I can sense His presence as if He is standing right beside me.

"'I believe the Creator has given us music as a way for us to enjoy that same intimacy with Him that you once enjoyed with Him in the garden. I know music isn't the only way we can be close to God, but I believe He has given it to us as an additional way to worship Him.'"

Abot concluded his story about Enosh by saying, "I don't believe the descendants of Cain realized the Creator's purpose for the gift of music, but He has given it to us through them, nonetheless. It is a reminder that God works His will through all things – even when we don't realize it!"

As I returned home that afternoon, I reflected on all the stories Abot had told me over the past several weeks. I thought they were interesting, and I valued the time I spent with him – but I questioned the relevance of his stories to my life.

"Enoch, where have you been all day?" my father asked when I got home.

After I explained, he asked, "What do you think of Abot's stories?"

"I'm not sure what to think," I replied. "I know he believes them to be true – and in some ways, I want them to be true. But I am struggling to believe in a God who would allow His creation to disobey Him and then punish them for doing so. If He is truly God, couldn't He have stopped them from disobeying Him?"

"That is a very good question, my son. There is no doubt they are wonderful stories crafted by Abot to explain the events of his life. But Abot is very old, and I sometimes wonder how much of his story is real and how much is imagined," my father said. "You must come to that decision on your own as well – and you have plenty of time to decide."

12

A DARE AND A SNAKE

~

*A*s the years passed, my brother Shep and I became fearless explorers. Our favorite spot was the hills and mountains on the east side of the river. We liked to climb to the highest peak and look out over the land. From there we could see across the western side of the valley all the way to the Euphrates River. It was a breathtaking sight.

The western face of the highest peak was a sheer drop of approximately 200 feet to a gradual slope. We normally hiked along the eastern path leading to the peak. But for some time now, Shep and I had been talking about climbing up the rocky face. After all, he and I were now fifteen and sixteen, respectively. We had often heard our older brothers bragging about climbing it. It almost seemed to be a rite of passage.

Whenever our mother heard any of us talking about it, she always forbade us from doing so. "I do not want you risking your lives over something that frivolous," she said on more than one occasion. But all of us boys just smiled and nodded. Sometimes our father would also add a halfhearted reprimand, but when our mother turned away, he would give us a wink.

Working in the fields each day kept Shep and me in pretty good physical shape. We also enjoyed a healthy brotherly competition. One day, we decided it was time for us to take on the rocky climb, and our conversation quickly turned into a challenge. I'm not sure who dared whom first, but it didn't take long before our minds were made up.

Since I was the older brother, I began my climb first. I was grateful to find there were plenty of cracks, lumps, and rough edges to provide hand and toe holds – just as our older brothers had said there would be. Once I had made it halfway to the top, Shep began his climb.

Periodically, I looked down to make certain my brother was all right. I eventually made it to the peak and pulled myself up onto the overlook. I then started watching my brother and shouting words of encouragement.

The last fifteen feet of the climb were actually the easiest. The angle was less severe and the ledges in the face were wider. Once Shep made it that far, we both began to celebrate our accomplishment. The anxiety we had stoically kept to ourselves was now behind us. We began to laugh and rehearse the words we were going to say to our older brothers later that night.

As Shep neared the overlook, he reached to take hold of the next ledge above him. Just then, a snake neither of us had seen struck and embedded its fangs in Shep's hand. He cried out in pain, but the greater challenge came from the fact that the snake had startled him. He lost his grip on the ledge and his one foot slipped off his toe hold. Though I attempted to grasp his hand, he was just beyond my reach. I watched in horror as my brother began free falling to the ground. He tried to grab a hand hold but failed.

His body hit the ground with a loud crack, immediately followed by an even louder thud as his head hit a rock.

"Shep!" I screamed at him over and over, willing him to respond. I knew the fastest way down was the path on the backside of the peak, so I took off running as fast as I could. It still took me five minutes to reach my brother.

As soon as I saw Shep's crumpled body up close, I knew he was dead. Ironically, the snake still had hold of Shep's hand and was lying lifeless beneath my brother's body, crushed by his weight as he landed on top of the snake with full force. For a moment, Abot's words about the head of the snake being crushed by his offspring echoed in my mind.

As I stood there, the magnitude of what had just happened crashed over me. My brother was dead . . . because of a meaningless dare. Sure, his fall had been an accident, and the dare had been mutual, but I still felt responsible. I dreaded facing my mother with the news. But more than anything, I grieved over losing my brother and my best friend. A life that should have lasted for centuries was snuffed out after fifteen short years.

Abot's story about Cain came to mind. I wondered if Cain had grieved for his younger brother, Abel. In Cain's case, it hadn't been an accident; it had been at his own hand. But had he ever felt any grief? I couldn't imagine what my life would be now without Shep, my closest confidant. Surely Cain must have felt something.

All of these thoughts were colliding in my mind – grief without comfort, questions without answers, and pain without relief. Suddenly, I cried out, "God of Abot! Where were You when the snake bit Shep's hand? Where were You when he fell to his death?

"Where were You when the snake convinced Matre and Abot to disobey You? Where were You when they fell from the paradise of that garden into this thorny and difficult world? Couldn't You have saved them? Couldn't You have saved Shep? Or is Your goodness just a wonderful story Abot made up? I think I will place my faith in the river god. At least I know where he is!"

I found some branches and created a stretcher to carry my brother's body back home. The heaviness of the journey was overwhelming – not from the weight of my brother, but from the weight of my grief.

13

WALKS THROUGH THE WOODS

～

My life wasn't the same after that day. Whenever I closed my eyes, I saw Shep's frightened expression as he struggled to grasp my outstretched hand. I blamed myself for his death, and though they never said it out loud, I believe my parents blamed me as well. There was a hole in my heart no one else would ever be able to fill.

I did not return to those hills; in fact, I stopped exploring east of the river altogether. I tried to compensate by spending more time working in the fields. I rationalized that I needed to make up for the fact there was one less worker now. I also discovered that if I kept busy, it distracted me from thinking about Shep.

Though Abot and Matre still lived nearby, I no longer visited them. Somehow the memory of Abot's stories made the pain of Shep's death even worse. Plus, I was convinced their God had been unable to prevent my brother's death. Either He did not have the power – or He just didn't care.

I became a loner. When I wasn't working, I frequently went for long solitary walks through the woods. During one of my meanderings, I encountered a girl named Dayana who told me she was lost. I didn't know her well but had occasionally seen her in the village. She was unsure how to get back home and asked if I would help her.

"I'm not headed home just yet, and I really don't want to talk right now," I replied. "But if you are agreeable to walking along with me in silence, our path will eventually lead back to your home."

She agreed and never once broke the silence. When we arrived back at her home, she told me she had enjoyed our walk and asked if we could do it again. To my own surprise, I agreed.

That became the first of many silent walks we took together. After a while, I found myself enjoying having a silent walking companion. Eventually, we even started to talk during those walks. She wasn't a chatterbox like most girls I knew, and I soon learned that when she spoke, it was always with purpose.

We discovered we were distant cousins with the same great-grandfather. I also found out she knew about Shep's death, as did most of the village. But, to her credit, she never asked me any questions about that day; rather, she allowed me to tell her what happened – over time, at my own pace.

After I had finished telling her the entire story during one of our walks, she looked into my eyes and said, "Enoch, Shep's death was a tragic accident, but it wasn't your fault. He wouldn't want you to live out the rest of your life believing you were responsible for his death. You both chose to climb that mountain. You both knew it was dangerous, but Shep chose to take the risk just like you did."

My parents and family had told me the same thing, but for almost four years I had refused to believe them . . . until that moment. Somehow,

Dayana penetrated the walls I had built around my heart. I accepted her words, and the grief that had been dammed up for all those years suddenly came spilling out.

I dropped to my knees and began to weep. I had never shed a tear over Shep in front of anyone else. But somehow, I felt safe to cry in front of Dayana. She took my hands in hers, but she didn't say a word. She permitted me to be vulnerable in the comfort of her silence.

I would like to say my heart opened up to my parents and the rest of my family after that day – but it did not. I still felt like they blamed me for Shep's death. But I did allow Dayana in, and she has owned a place in my heart ever since.

Two years later, we became husband and wife. Abot, Matre, and all our family joined in our marriage celebration. That night as we all sat around the fire, Abot and Matre told us about their early days in Eden. "Toward the end of each day," Abot began, "the Creator would often invite us to join Him for a walk around the garden. Each time, He took us to a place in the garden we had never seen before, and we marveled at its beauty. The Creator explained every detail – why He had chosen each shape, each color, and each design.

"He told us that nothing had been left to chance. He designed and created each and every detail. And He reminded us that at the end of each day of creation, He had seen that everything was good and perfect."

We all listened respectfully to Abot, though none of us truly believed in the Creator. By this time, everyone viewed his stories as fascinating folklore. Dayana and I did agree about the beauty his stories described. We had seen that same beauty ourselves during our many frequent walks – even if we weren't in Eden.

Abot challenged us all, just as he always did, to turn our hearts back to the Creator. "Heed my words of truth! Do not worship those things He created, worship Him – the only One who is worthy of worship!" he declared. But like always, his impassioned plea fell on deaf ears and hardened hearts.

One year later, my oldest son, Aviv, was born. His name means "the beginning of spring." Since he was to be our firstborn of many to come, we thought it was an appropriate name. As the years passed, Dayana and I had many more sons and daughters. As our family grew, we had less time for our evening strolls through the woods. We missed those times together.

14

THE SONS OF CAIN

~

*A*s the descendants of Adam continued to multiply, it was necessary for families and tribes to migrate to distant regions to find fertile land on which to settle and grow their food. Inevitably, that caused increased conflict as tribes began to settle in regions already claimed by other tribes.

We were hearing reports that large bands of robbers from the east, descendants of Cain, were attacking villages down river from us where Seth's descendants lived. Cain's people intended to wrestle control of the land by driving away the current occupants – through intimidation or death, whichever they deemed necessary.

So far, our village had been left alone. We weren't certain if they were avoiding us out of respect for Abot and Matre living here, or they just hadn't made their way to us yet. Regardless, we knew we could not sit idly by as our cousins were being attacked. We discovered the marauders were under the leadership of Obal, the tenth generation from Adam and the great grandson of Tubal-cain.

My father assembled our entire family and announced, "We must take up arms and help our extended family defend their villages against these bandits. Some of our men will remain here to defend our village, while the rest will go to aid the other villages."

Abot stood up and declared, "I will pray that the Creator goes before you and gives you victory over the evil intentions of the sons of Cain. I know you are farmers and not fighting men, but Jehovah God will fight for you!"

As we studied how Obal had defeated the villages, there was no question his planned attacks were strategic. Though the villages were each surrounded by protective walls, they obviously had not provided a good defense. We learned that Obal frequently led his attacks at first light while the village was still sleeping. The villagers would wake up disoriented and ill-prepared. We realized if we were going to defeat Obal, we would need to catch him off guard.

He would be expecting a frontal assault at his camp, so our best option was to surprise him when he was preparing to attack. Based on his attack pattern, we knew his next target was one of three villages. So, we needed to be prepared to launch counterattacks in those places.

My father divided our fighting force into thirds and chose two of my older brothers and me to each lead one of those divisions. I was given the responsibility of defending the village of Larak, named for one of Seth's grandsons. Jobab was the leader of the village. He and his sons and grand-sons were brave men with an unbendable resolve to defend their village at all costs.

Jobab and I agreed on a strategy to defeat Obal if he attacked. After the sun set, we positioned our best archers at the most strategic vantage points in the tree line outside the village gate and on top of the village walls. I instructed them to remain out of sight and not release their arrows until they heard my signal.

At the same time, we positioned half of the remaining men with clubs and spears in the brush scattered throughout the forest; the rest of the men were stationed behind the city gate. They, too, were to stay hidden until they heard my signal.

Now came the hardest part – we needed to be alert and silent throughout the night to watch for Obal and his men. Our men posted at the two other villages saw nothing but the morning sun shining on an empty plain. But my men were rewarded with the arrival of Obal and his men walking right into our trap.

They stealthily approached the city, assuming the village was unprepared for their arrival. On my signal, our archers' arrows rained down on the attacking force from behind and above. Obal's men were out in the open and had nowhere to hide. They hastily retreated as our men behind the gate and in the brush assaulted them with spears and clubs.

Our men stood firm and fought bravely, and the fight was over in short order. Obal suffered an overwhelming defeat that day. Though I was grateful for our victory, I couldn't ignore the fact that we were family fighting family. Just as Cain had killed his brother, cousin was turned against cousin. And I feared this would not be the last time family blood was spilled.

I thought about what Abot said before we left our village to fight this battle. Had the Creator truly fought for us? All of Obal's men had died in the battle – but not one of our men perished! Jobab led his people to offer sacrifices to the sun god for his help in our victory. I, however, attributed the victory to our well-executed strategy.

In the days that followed, we remained watchful, doubting that the sons of Cain would halt their efforts because of one defeat. However, they made no further advances. It would be years before I discovered what caused their full retreat. Just as it would be years before I would truly understand what happened that day. But one thing I knew with certainty – the sun god had nothing to do with it!

15

AND THEN I WALKED WITH GOD

~

*W*hen I was sixty-five years old, Dayana announced that we were expecting another child. The births of our last three children had taken a toll on her physically, so I was concerned for her welfare.

From the first day we met, I learned that Dayana's eyes were the window to her soul. I could often tell what she was thinking by just looking into her eyes. And they were telling me she was weak and worried.

As time for the baby's arrival approached, so did the time for the first harvest of the year – which meant presenting our harvest offering to the river god. I had always asked the river god for a good yield, as well as health and prosperity. This time I decided I would ask him for strength and health for Dayana as she delivered our child. I made sure our offering was the absolute best of the best. I wanted the river god to be so pleased with me that he would not hesitate to grant my request.

Three days after I presented the offering, Dayana went into labor. I sent word to two women in our camp who were going to assist with the birth. After a short while, one of the women came to me and whispered, "Your wife does not look good. I fear she will not survive this birth."

"Oh yes, she will!" I replied. "I presented an excellent offering to the river god, and I am certain he will answer my request."

"I fear he will not," she answered, before returning to my wife.

At that moment, Abot and Matre arrived at our tent. "Enoch," Abot said, "we hear that your wife is about to give birth. We have come to extend our congratulations to you both!"

"We thank you for your good wishes," I replied, "but the baby has not yet arrived. And the midwives fear Dayana is not strong enough to deliver the child."

Matre hurriedly left to go to my wife. Abot motioned for me to sit down as he said, "I will pray with you to the Creator that He will give Dayana the strength to endure the pain and suffering of childbirth."

But before he could pray, Matre returned to tell us, "Dayana is at death's door. There is nothing any of us can do. We must pray that the Lord God Creator will heal her and strengthen her so she and the child might live."

 "I prayed to the river god," I cried out, "but he did not answer me! If your God, the Creator, will have mercy on us and answer our prayer, I will turn to Him and follow Him alone for the rest of my days!"

All three of us knelt, and Abot began to pray. When he finished, I began. "Creator, I do not know You the way Abot does. I have denied Your existence most of my life. I have looked elsewhere to find You. I have looked to Your creation and denied Your power. I have accepted lies and denied Your truth. Forgive me, Oh God, for my sins. Forgive me for my faithlessness. I do not deserve Your mercy, but still I ask You to extend it. Today I turn to walk with You. Heal my wife and allow her and my child to live . . ."

Just then my prayer was interrupted by the sound of a baby's cry! Matre quickly went to check on Dayana. I continued to pray to the Creator while she was gone. The next sound I heard was not a baby's cry, it was the voice of the Creator – not audibly – but in my spirit saying, "Enoch, I have heard your cry and I have answered your prayer. Your wife lives and so does your child. Your child will be a sign to you and all of the people.

"There is a judgment coming to all of the people because of their wickedness and sinfulness. The day is coming when I will destroy every living thing. But I will hold off that judgment for as long as this child lives. He is my gift to you and Dayana, and the years of his life will be a gift to those who choose to follow Me. You will be My prophet and deliver My message of salvation to the people."

Just then Matre returned and told me to go see my wife. As I turned the corner, I saw my wife sitting up holding our baby. Dayana looked at me and smiled. The weakness I had seen earlier had been replaced with the joy and strength she usually exhibited. Gone was any sign of illness. Her health and strength had fully returned.

She turned our son's face toward me and said, "Enoch, meet your newest son! What should we call him?"

"His name will be Methuselah," I answered, "which means 'his death will send.' The Creator has told me our son will live a long life, but the judgment of God will be ushered in on the day of his death. His life will be a sign that the Creator has extended His mercy, but He will not withhold His judgment forever."

That was the day that changed my life. The Creator, by His mercy, spared my wife's life. He gave us many more years together, and together Dayana and I worshiped Him. He gave us a son – a son with a promise – for us and for all mankind. As wonderful as all of those precious gifts were to me that day, He gave me one more gift – one that was even greater. He gave me the gift of His presence. He granted me the privilege of walking with Him, just as Abot had once walked with Him. He granted me the gift of knowing Him intimately and speaking His truth. My life would never be the same!

16

A STILL, SMALL VOICE

~

*W*hen I told Dayana how I had prayed to the Creator and how He had answered my prayer, she, too, asked Him to forgive her sins. There was so much we had to learn and understand about Him and He patiently taught us. I also sought forgiveness from Abot and Matre for the disrespect I had shown them. They became a great encouragement to Dayana and me in our walk with God.

One of the greatest sorrows in my life is the fact that most of my older children did not turn to God. The sins and lies I lived out during my younger years greatly influenced them. They refused to accept the truth of a loving Creator who desired for them to have a relationship with Him. They blamed Him for all the evil in the world and rejected my pleas for them to repent. The Lord God had called me to be His prophet, but even my own children were refusing to heed the words of truth He was giving me to declare.

In the days immediately following Methuselah's birth, the Lord invited me to go on long walks with Him. He directed where He would have me go as we spoke. One day He invited me to cross the river and walk with Him through the land surrounding the mountain where Shep had died. I vehemently shook my head and told Him, "I can't go there!"

"Enoch, there are many places I will lead you as you walk with Me," the Creator said. "You must trust Me and know that I will never leave you nor forsake you. Some of the places I lead will be difficult for you. Some will involve giants from your past that I will lead you to conquer like this mountain. Trust Me no matter what it is. I will always have a purpose in it all!"

God was not only teaching Dayana and me, He was also teaching Methuselah even though he was just a lad. When Methuselah was six years old, he asked me, "Father, I hear you carrying on conversations with God, but the only one I ever hear is you. I can't see God or hear Him speaking back to you. Can you see or hear Him?"

"I don't always see Him with my eyes," I answered, "but I sense His presence, just as surely as I know you are right here with me."

"But, Father," he replied, "do you hear His voice?"

"He speaks to me in a still, small voice," I said. "I don't hear Him with my ears. I hear Him with my heart, and my spirit bears witness to all that He tells me."

"Have you ever seen Him with your eyes, Father?" Methuselah asked.

I nodded as I answered him, "Yes, on occasion He comes to me in person and invites me to walk with Him in the gardens like He once did with Abot."

My heart leapt for joy when he asked, "Father, can I join you when you go for walks with God?"

"That is up to the Creator," I replied. "He alone chooses how we enter into His presence. It's not because of who our family is, or even what we have done. He only chooses those who ask for His forgiveness and honestly seek Him and acknowledge who He is by faith. That is called living righteously, and though many may try to convince others through their actions that they are righteous, the Creator sees our hearts. He alone knows whose heart is truly turned toward Him."

"I want my heart to be truly turned toward Him," Methuselah declared with all the sincerity a little boy could muster.

"I know you do," I said. "And I pray that will always be the case. God has promised me you will be saved from the judgment that will one day come to this earth. Your death will be a signal that the time of judgment has come. I fear the days will become even more evil as that day approaches. I have asked the Creator to help you walk righteously before Him in the midst of that evil."

Our conversation was interrupted as we returned to the village. "We will continue this conversation another day," I told him. "Continue to seek Him and honor Him with all of your heart."

As the years passed, Methuselah developed an interest in carving wood. One day, while he was walking through the woods, he came upon a thick branch lying on the ground. As he stared at it, he began to imagine it was a panther crouched low to the ground and hunting for prey.

He picked up the branch and began to break off the portions of wood that were not part of his mental picture. Soon he realized he needed to use an instrument of some kind to create more delicate lines in the wood. He pulled out the small knife I had recently made for Him.

He sat down and began to carve. The more he carved, the more the piece of wood began to look like the panther in his mind. When he arrived home, he showed me what he had made. The carving was beautiful. I was amazed at the workmanship he demonstrated on his first effort at carving. I told him that clearly God had given him a gift to reflect the magnificence of creation through his woodwork.

But I was even more proud when he said, "The Creator told me in His still, small voice that carving is a lot like what He does in each of our lives. He has an image in His mind of what He intends for each of us to look like as we follow Him. He is patiently removing the large chunks and the small pieces from our lives that don't align with that image.

"It often hurts when He removes the larger chunks – and sometimes there is pain when He takes away the smaller pieces. But we need to trust that He knows what He is doing. He knows the image He is conforming us into!"

My son was becoming my teacher!

~

17

THE SERPENT'S BITE

⁓

$\mathcal{A}$s the years went by, Methuselah continued to practice and fine tune his wood-carving skills. He carved so many animals he could no longer think of one he had not chiseled. He asked Abot to describe more animals to him. Soon, many of the villagers were asking him to carve a bird or an animal for them. It was becoming a profitable skill.

In his late teens, Methuselah's eye was drawn to a girl named Mira, who was about his age and lived in our village. They began to take long walks together through the woods. One late afternoon as they were walking, Methuselah noticed a large, uniquely shaped tree branch on the ground. It was a size and shape he knew would produce a beautiful carving. As he reached down to pick it up, a snake appeared from the back side of it and lunged at his hand. It embedded its fangs deep into his flesh and held fast. Methuselah reached down with his other hand, picked up the piece of wood, and struck the snake. It released its hold and fell to the ground. Methuselah clubbed it to death with the large branch.

The area surrounding the two puncture wounds in his hand quickly began to turn red. He and Mira knew from the snake's markings that the bite was poisonous. They also knew a bite like this often leads to death – and there is no known cure.

Methuselah had the presence of mind to turn to his source of hope. He called out to the Creator, "Lord God, the venom from this snake is one of the consequences of the deceitful actions of the serpent in the Garden of Eden. But just as You were able to cause that serpent and all that would follow him to slither on the ground, You are able to remove the poisonous effects of this one's venom. You have promised that I will live a long and fruitful life – and I trust You for the fulfillment of that promise."

As Mira and Methuselah watched, the redness on his hand began to disappear. The pain subsided, and in a few moments the puncture wounds closed. The only evidence he had been bitten was the dead snake on the ground. The Creator had heard his prayer and healed him!

Methuselah brought the dead snake back to camp as evidence of what had just taken place. He intended for everyone in the village to hear the news of what the Creator had done. No one would be able to deny His power! "Our God is faithful!" he exclaimed to all who listened.

I sent word to Abot since I knew he would want to hear what the Lord God Creator had done. Though he was now 707 years old, Abot still had the strength of his younger days, and his resolve to honor the Creator in all things had not diminished. He joined his voice in praise over the goodness of God to my son.

"Just as the Lord God Creator promised," Abot said, "the serpent's head has again been crushed! Praise be to the One who is God over all. Though the evil one attempted to destroy this one who has been given as a reminder of God's mercy and grace, the Creator's might and power have proven that His promises will always be fulfilled. The evil one is a defeated foe!"

"But Abot," Methuselah asked, "how did the evil one ever come to be?"

"He was the most beautiful of God's creations," Abot replied. "He was created by God as a guardian cherub named Lucifer. He was *the signet of perfection, full of wisdom, and perfect in beauty.*[1] He was appointed to be the guardian over the Garden of Eden. But he rebelled against God. He was no longer content to be the most beautiful and most powerful created being; rather, he wanted to be God. He did not want to worship God, he wanted to be worshiped.

"That's why he came to Matre that day. He decided that if he could get God's creation to turn away from our Creator, he would prove himself to be greater than the Creator – he would be in the position of God. But the fact is, no matter how much he may want to be God, he never will be! He is a created being who will be judged and punished for his evil.

"The Creator cast him down from heaven and promised that He will send One who will ultimately defeat the evil one and redeem us from our sins. He will then reign over the earth and cast the evil one and those who have followed him into eternal damnation. And that Savior will come through our offspring. He will be born from my ancestral line. He will be born from your ancestral line, Methuselah. That's why he sought to kill you and made a feeble attempt to prevent God from accomplishing His purpose through your life. But He is a defeated foe, just like this dead snake lying on the ground!"

Though the evil one's attempt to destroy my son had been defeated, we knew he was still at work to corrupt the descendants of Adam. Word had already reached us that other angelic beings who had chosen to follow the evil one now walked the earth. They had first arrived in the land called Nod – the land inhabited by the descendants of Cain. There they saw the beautiful women of the human race and took those they chose to be their wives.

I declared to all who were gathered, "The Creator has told me that the evil one continues to prowl the earth in his effort to accomplish his evil intent. He has apparently decided that if the Savior will be a descendant of Abot, he will attempt to foil the plan by corrupting the entire human race – not only through our sin nature, but also through the intermarriage of his demonic angels with the daughters of Adam and Eve.

"The Creator told me the evil one believes that if he infects the entire human race through his demonic beings, there will be no line through which the Savior can be born. But, as always, the evil one has underestimated the Sovereign and Almighty God! His purpose and plan will not be thwarted – that which He has put in motion will be accomplished!"

∾

18

THE SONS OF GOD

～

*I*n the days that followed, we heard additional reports of the evil deeds of the fallen angels. The Creator had shown me that the greatest weapon wielded by the evil one was the weapon of deceit. Sadly, he had used that weapon quite effectively to lead Abot and Matre astray in the garden, and he had continued to use it successfully ever since.

But his efforts were not limited solely to the descendants of Adam here on earth; he employed that same weapon to enlist the complicity of the sons of God – the angels in heaven. While they were still yet in heaven, before the Lord God cast them out, the evil one craftily deceived many of the angels with promises of personal power and gain. Angels cannot see into the future any more than the evil one can, so many of them had blindly fallen prey to his wiles.

As time passed, the evil one pointed out the beauty of the growing number of daughters of Cain and introduced the seed of lustful desire and thoughts into their hearts. In heaven the angels had never engaged in sexual relations, nor had they ever had any desire. The thought of doing so went against everything they had known since the Lord God had created them. Though they were fallen angels, they still had some understanding of right and wrong.

But the evil one would not be put off by their apprehension. He decided to raise up an accomplice from among their number with the promise of increased power in the evil one's kingdom on earth. The evil one established a fallen angel named Semjaza as a leader over them all and instructed him on how to lead the others to act on their lustful desires.

Semjaza stood before the other fallen angels and said, "Come, let us choose wives from among the children of men who will bear children unto us, as our master, Lucifer, has instructed us to do. I fear you will not agree to do what he has asked, and I alone will have to pay the penalty for this great sin. But I question if there is truly a penalty, or rather is it a prize we have been denied? The Creator has given this pleasure to men; why should it not also be ours?"[1]

After a moment's hesitation, the multitude answered back in unison, "Let us all swear an oath, and bind ourselves by a mutual curse not to abandon this plan but to do this thing."[1] They bound themselves with full knowledge of their sin and chose to take wives from the daughters of men.

They taught their wives charms, enhancements, and how to practice other forms of divination. The evil that had begun among men in the Garden of Eden was now being escalated beyond description. And in the midst of this evil, they bore a race of giants who, in turn, furthered the evil practices introduced by their progenitors.

However, the depravity did not stop there. When the daughters of men could no longer satisfy their desires and the sons of men could no longer sustain them, the giants turned against them and began to devour mankind. Their deviant practices soon involved all manner of evil against all living things. But still their thirst for evil would not be quenched. They began to devour one another's flesh and drink the blood.

The Lord looked down at the wickedness that now extended throughout His creation and was sorry He had ever made any of it – the created beings that had fallen from heaven and mankind who now occupied the earth.

One day as I was walking with Him, He declared, *"I will completely wipe out this human race that I have created. Yes, and I will destroy all the animals and birds, too. I am sorry I ever made them!"* (2)

My heart was broken over His anguish, and I suddenly found myself thinking, "Lord, will you destroy both the innocent and guilty alike?" But I didn't merely think those words, I suddenly realized I had spoken them out loud!

I had never before questioned God about anything He said He was going to do. I did not know how He would react. After all, who am I to question the Sovereign and Almighty God? Where was I when He created the world? Who am I to question the One who spoke the sky, the land, and the seas into existence? How could I even pretend to question the One who created the very beings that He now determined He would need to destroy?

Besides, are any of us truly innocent? We have all come from the seed of Adam. We are all sinners. Why should we presume that the Creator spare any of us?

But then I heard Him speak. "I will spare those who are righteous from the wrath of My judgment," He said. "I will remove them from this earth before I unleash my judgment.

"I will be gracious and faithful to them, just as I have been to you. On the day you led your men to attack the forces of Obal at Larkin, I was there with you. Even though you denied My existence and My power, I was gracious to you and spared the lives of all of your men. How much more will I be faithful to those who turn their hearts to Me!

"And even in the midst of My judgment, I will spare one man and his family from death. He will be a righteous man through whom I will replenish the earth as I intended."

"Lord, when will this be and who is this man?" I asked.

"It is for Me only to know the time. But I have given you a promise that your son Methuselah will not die until that day of judgment has arrived. And the one through whom I will replenish the earth will be of his seed – your seed, Enoch!

'Now, you must be about the work I have given you. You are not to invest your time worrying when I will bring judgment or how I will do so. Your work is to call those who will respond to repentance! Make haste, Enoch, for the day of judgment will come soon!"

∽

19

SHARED JOY . . . AND SHARED SORROW

~

*W*hen I was 252 years old, Methuselah and Mira were blessed with a son they named Lamech, which means strong and vigorous. The Creator gave me three promises regarding my grandson: He would walk in righteousness before His God. He would be saved from the coming day of judgment. And the Savior whom God would one day send to earth would be born through Lamech's ancestral line.

The day Methuselah and Mira dedicated Lamech to the Lord, Dayana, Abot, Matre, and I stood by their sides. It was then the Lord gave me one more promise. He said Lamech would live a long life – and Methuselah would be there to walk beside him each and every day.

When Lamech was old enough to understand, his father and I told him of God's promise that the Savior of the world would come from his lineage. I was proud of his understanding and spiritual maturity when he asked, "Why am I in that line? What have I done – or what could I ever do – that is so outstanding I would be considered worthy to be part of God's eternal plan?"

"You have done nothing to earn God's favor," I said. "It is God's mercy and grace extended to you. You do not walk with God out of privilege, you walk with Him by faith!"

From an early age, Lamech demonstrated carpentry skills, just like his father. Until my son's generation, each of us had primarily been farmers who also did everything else needed to provide for our families. But in more recent years, many had begun taking on a trade using their unique talent and skills.

People would then barter their trade for the goods or services provided by others. It became a more efficient way to glean what was needed, and everyone felt more fulfilled doing the work they enjoyed. Some of my sons and grandsons cultivated the land like my father had done, and others became capable hunters, pottery makers, tanners, weavers, and the like.

When Lamech turned eighteen, his parents arranged for him to marry a young woman named Shira who lived in our village. Her name means singing, and she truly brought music into our lives. God soon blessed them with a home full of children.

When I was 282 years old, our family experienced a difficult loss. We always knew the day would come, but that didn't make us any more prepared. Matre died at the age of 900. She was the matriarch of us all. Her family numbered more than anyone could count. Some said it was in the billions; I don't know about that, but it was definitely a lot!

Obviously, the one most affected by her death was Abot. She was bone of his bone and flesh of his flesh. They had been husband and wife for every day of their lives. They alone shared the memory of Eden. They alone had seen the sun rise and set every day since the beginning.

None of us could imagine their shared joys – or their shared sorrows. We would never know the weight they carried because they ushered sin into the world. None of us would ever enjoy the simplicity of life unburdened by the knowledge of good and evil. And we would never experience walking in fellowship with God without any element of sin to separate us.

Death is a reminder of sin. The Creator never intended for us to experience physical death. Our bodies were never intended to grow old. The ages of all of our patriarchs, including this generation, were a constant reminder of God's original intention. But recently God had told me, *"My Spirit will no longer put up with humans for such a long time, for they are mortal flesh. In the future they will live no more than 120 years."* [1]

Today, 120 years is considered young, but one day soon that age will be considered very old, which means the aging process we all go through will accelerate. Even though God said it, it was still hard for me to imagine at the age of 282 what that would be like.

Though we sent out word to many other villages and cities about Matre's death, few of her descendants knew of her passing, and even fewer grieved her death. Many probably didn't even know her name.

Members of my family – including Seth and Chava, together with their son, Enosh, and his wife – traveled to our village to pay their respects. Seth was now 770 and Enosh was 665, so travel was difficult for them. None of Matre's other sons came, and we didn't think any of them were walking righteously before God. Sadly, that was a sorrow most of us as parents could understand.

Soon after the mourning period was over, I suggested to Abot that he move in with Lamech and Shira. It would be good for him to be surrounded by their happy family, and it would be an honor and privilege for them to care for him.

I knew this was another reminder that the day of judgment was coming soon.

20

THE SECOND ADAM

~

*J*n the days that followed, the Lord took me to a place I had never been before. He said it would one day be called Horeb – the mountain of God. As I knelt before Him, He allowed me to see a vision: the Creator took me into the heavens where I saw One whose countenance was that of a Man with a kind face.

I asked one of the heavenly hosts standing near to me who the Man was, and he replied, "This is the Promised One – the Son of Man – who is and was and forever will be. Yea, before the sun and the stars were created, His name was named. He shall be a staff to the righteous, light to the Gentiles, and the hope of those who are troubled of heart. All who dwell on earth shall one day fall down and worship Him with praise and blessing and celebration.[1]

"And on that day, the earth will give back that which has been entrusted to it, Sheol will give back that which it has received, and hell will give back that which it owes. For in those days, the Son of Man will arise, and He will choose the elect from among them for the day will have drawn nigh that they should be delivered.[1]

"And the Son of Man will in those days sit on the Creator's throne, and His mouth will pour forth all wisdom, counsel, and judgment. The earth will rejoice, the righteous will dwell upon it, and the elect will walk there-on."[1]

The Lord God Creator permitted me to see all the secrets of the heavens, how the kingdom is divided, and how the actions of men are weighed in the balance. I saw the mansions of the elect and the mansions of the heavenly hosts. My eyes saw all the sinners being cast away into the punishment they will be forced to endure forever.

Then I looked down and saw a deep valley with fire where the sinners were being cast. Beside the opening of the valley were iron chains of immeasurable weight. I asked the angel, "For whom are those chains being prepared?"[1]

He said to me, "These are being prepared to subdue the evil one and the angels who followed him just before they are cast into the abyss of complete condemnation. And their jaws will be covered with rough stones so they will not be able to utter another deceptive word. The angels of the Lord will take hold of them on that day and cast them into the burning furnace as their punishment for leading astray those who dwelt on the earth."[1]

When I awoke there on the mountain of Horeb, the Lord God Jehovah said to me, "Go and tell everyone what you have seen. Say unto them:

"Listen! The Lord is coming with countless thousands of His holy ones to execute judgment on the people of the world. He will convict every person of all the ungodly things they have done and for all the insults that ungodly sinners have spoken against Him."[2]

In the blink of an eye, He delivered me to a hillside overlooking a city where I now stood alone. However, He left no doubt as to what I was to do and say:

"Hear, you men of old, and see, you that have come after, the words of the Holy One which I have been sent to declare . . ."

I then proceeded to proclaim everything God had permitted me to see.

When I was 308 years old, Abot died. He was 930 years of age. Though a few of his descendants would live longer than he did, none of them would ever experience what he had during his lifetime.

As I helped prepare his body for burial, I lingered a moment as I saw the scar God left when He removed the rib from which He formed Matre. As I saw his stomach, I was again reminded by the absence of a navel that Abot had never been inside a mother's womb. He had experienced things the rest of us would never know.

In his later years, Abot and I often talked about the privilege God had given both of us to walk with Him. Abot always looked sad when he said those words, because he knew his sin had cost him that privilege. But then he would smile as he looked at me and say, "Enoch, the Creator has given you the privilege of walking with Him as a friend walks with a friend. Do not ever do anything to lose that privilege. No relationship can ever replace it."

Abot had taught me more than any other man in my life. Of all of the millions – or billions – of his descendants still living, he chose to invest his life in mine. I could have been like so many and never really known him. But through his effort and by God's grace that wasn't the case. I would miss him greatly. But I knew better than most that I would see him again one day.

The first Adam would live again – because the One who would become known as the second Adam would one day come to earth to make that possible! And both Adams would share one important distinction – neither was created through the seed of an earthly father!

As word spread throughout cities and villages that Abot had died, the whole earth stopped to honor him and mourn his passing. A week of mourning was declared to grieve his death. For those few brief days, the righteous and unrighteous came together in a single purpose. It was said that those days of mourning were the first and last days that all people united since that fateful day in the Garden of Eden. And I knew it would not occur again until the day the Second Adam comes to judge and reign over all the earth.

21

WALKING THROUGH THE DIFFICULT DAYS

~

"*M*ethuselah," I said, "call to me all of your sons. For the Word calls me, and the Spirit is poured out upon me, that I may show you and your children everything that shall befall you and the generations to come."[1]

When Methuselah's family had assembled, I declared, "Hear, you sons of Methuselah, all the words of your grandfather, and harken to my voice. I exhort you and say to you, beloved, love uprightness and walk therein. Do not be drawn away from uprightness by your deceitful hearts, and do not associate with those who are double-minded.[2]

"But walk in righteousness, my sons. It will guide you on right paths and lead you where you are to walk. Violence will increase on the earth and a great chastisement is coming soon. Yes, the earth will be cut off from its roots, and its whole structure will be destroyed. But you can yet escape that destruction. [2]

"In the days preceding the great chastisement, unrighteousness together with all of its deeds and violence will be on the increase, as will apostasy and transgression. Then the Holy Lord will pour out His wrath and chastisement to execute His judgment upon the earth.[2]

"The roots of unrighteousness and deceit will be destroyed. The idols of the heathen will be abandoned, their temples will be obliterated, and the unrighteous themselves will perish in judgment forever.[2]

"So now, harken unto me, my sons, and walk in the paths of righteousness. For all who walk in the paths of unrighteousness will perish in the judgment forever."[2]

But the only son of Methuselah who chose to walk in the path of integrity and honor was Lamech. Even Lamech's adult sons chose the paths of deception, trusting in their own riches and the false thinking of the world.

At the Creator's prompting, I continued to declare the warning of God's upcoming judgment to all men, but they responded much the same as the sons of Lamech. There was little question that only a few would follow the narrow path of righteousness leading up to the day God would cry out, "Enough!"

Dayana would often come to me and ask, "How much longer will the Creator delay in sending His judgment? Surely, He has extended mercy beyond all reason."

Each time I would reply, "He will delay His judgment until His perfect time has arrived. We cannot comprehend His ways. His grace and mercy are beyond anything we could ever understand. But let there be no doubt – the day of His judgment will arrive!"

God granted our family peace and safety despite the evil surrounding us. Though the people rejected their Creator, they felt some sense of respect for Abot and Matre.

We knew God was our protector, but our neighbors told us we would not be harmed because our family had cared for Abot and Matre in their final years. So, each day we walked through the fire of evil knowing God would keep even the clothes on our backs from being singed.

I have learned over the years that walking with God is rarely a serene, peaceful walk. It is a walk that requires faith and courage. He does not only lead me beside the still waters, but He also sometimes leads me through the raging fires and the howling winds. I have walked with Him to the highest peaks and surveyed His majesty, but I have also walked with Him to the lowest depths of anguish and death.

Knowing He was right by my side for every step is what has given me strength, comfort, and assurance. I have never needed to ask Him what step to take or where to go. I have learned if I keep my eyes on Him and remain by His side, He will always lead me to the exact spot He wants me to be – no matter how majestic, mundane, or terrifying.

Over the years, He has led me to confront murderers, sorcerers, and those who practice all manner of evil. He has led me to stand alone in the midst of evil doers who vehemently reject the message of repentance. But the most difficult place He has ever led me was to the bedside of my dying wife.

We had been married 342 years. I could barely remember a day when we were not together. We had walked with God hand in hand. We had encouraged one another when the journey was difficult, and we had celebrated with each other when the days were filled with overwhelming joy. I cried out to the Lord, just as I had done 295 years earlier.

"Lord, You answered my prayer even when I denied Your existence! You healed my wife and allowed her and my son to live. Would you do it again? Would you spare her life and permit us to live out our lives together? You know my frame! You know how much I depend on her. She is the helpmate You created for me. Spare her, Oh Lord!"

I felt His presence. I knew He was right there with me. His invitation to walk with Him all those years ago had also assured me He would always be with me. And this was one of those times.

I heard His reassuring voice as He said, "Enoch, it is time for her to die. She has completed her race, and she has finished well. I have more for you to do, which will not necessitate her being by your side. If you understood what that is, you would agree. But for now, you need to trust Me.

"Dayana is as much My child as you are. Believe it or not, I love her even more than you do. It is time for her to enter into her rest. It is time for you to let her go. You will see her again one day – and on that day there will be no more sadness and no more pain. In the meantime, trust Me to draw both of you close to Me."

I held the hands of my precious wife as our Creator permitted us one more treasured moment. Though her eyes had remained closed for several days, she opened them for one brief moment. As my eyes met hers, we said goodbye – not in words, but through our gaze . . . one I will hold in my heart until the day we again look upon one another.

22

DAYS OF MERCY AND GRACE

~

wo years after Dayana died, the Lord told me to go visit my ancestors, Seth (son of Adam) and Enosh (son of Seth). They were living in a village two days' journey downriver. I had last seen them fifty-four years earlier on the occasion of Abot's death. I didn't yet know why the Lord wanted us to visit them, but I knew He would show me in His perfect timing.

Seth and his wife, Chava, welcomed Methuselah, Lamech, and me with open arms, as did Enosh and his wife. The news of my warnings about God's coming judgment had reached their village. "Sadly," Seth told us, "most of our neighbors view your warnings as the rantings of a lunatic instead of a warning from the Almighty God. And they no longer listen to the melodies of worship that Enosh sings. Instead of being moved to repentance and worship, they mock the words – and worse, they mock the Lord God Creator.

"I count it a blessing that you three men are walking with God. Most of those here in our village are also my descendants, and my heart aches that they, like many others, have turned their backs on our Creator."

"Sadly, that is also true of my father (Jared) and my grandfather (Mahalalel), who are also your direct descendants," I said.

"And it is true of my son (Kenan), who is their immediate ancestor," Enosh replied.

"That means three of the men who stand between the three of us and the two of you generationally will enter into the judgment of God separated from Him if they continue to refuse to repent of their sins," I acknowledged.

"We must once more urge the three of them to turn from their wicked ways. I will summon them to come here for a gathering of their ancestral line from the second generation of Adam through the ninth," Seth declared. "They will not refuse an invitation for this once-in-a-lifetime gathering – a reunion of eight generations!"

He prepared messages and had them sent to the three men. By the end of the week all three had arrived in his village. The generations included:

Seth, aged 854,
Enosh, aged 749,
Kenan, aged 659,
Mahalalel, aged 589,
Jared, aged 524,
Me, aged 362,
Methuselah, aged 297, and
Lamech, aged 110.

"Sons, and sons of my sons," Seth began once we were all gathered, "we are the generations that followed our patriarch, Adam. We are the ancestral line through whom the One promised to Adam will one day come. We have been given the honor of bearing the seed of the One who will defeat the evil one deceiving our people.

"For this divine purpose, we should be men who walk righteously before God. And yet, some of you have chosen to pursue your own path and have disregarded the words of Adam. You have disregarded the one who knew better than any man the true cost of going your own way.

"You have heard Enoch deliver the warnings from our Creator. God has called him to be His prophet, bringing His message of the coming judgment to our wicked generations. And yet some of you have not heeded his warnings.

"What more do you men need? Your father, Adam, and one of your sons, Enoch, have both been used by God to call all people to repentance. You, who share their bloodline, should be the first to accept their words as truth. You men should be first among all men to walk righteously before our God and Creator.

"You men, above all others, have been blessed by God to be the bearers of His message. How can you obstinately turn your backs on Him and pursue your own evil ways? As your sole living patriarch, I beg you, as do Enosh and these three of your sons – Enoch, Methuselah, and Lamech. Repent of your wickedness, turn back to your Creator, and live righteously so you might escape the coming judgment. And urge your offspring to do the same."

I would like to tell you my great-grandfather, my grandfather and my father all repented that day and made the decision to walk honorably before God – but they did not. They all told Seth they would consider his words and my message of repentance and decide for themselves. I never saw a change in my father's or grandfather's actions, so I fear they did not. I do not know what my great-grandfather chose to do.

But Seth and I were obedient to what God directed us to do by giving our family members one more opportunity to repent. I never saw Seth, Enosh, or Kenan again, but I had a peace knowing I had done what God wanted me to do. He reminded me – that just like all people – they needed to decide for themselves. No one escapes the judgment of God because their parent or grandparent walked righteously with God. Each one must choose.

A few months later, God took me to a high peak on the mountains of Ararat. As I looked out over the expanse of land, God told me, "The days of mercy and grace I have extended to this evil generation are coming to an end. One day soon I will cover the earth with a flood that will destroy every living thing. Everything on earth will die. But I will raise up a remnant from your seed and keep him and his family safe from the flood waters in a boat I will direct him to build. They will bring a pair of every living animal and bird into the boat to keep them alive as well."[1]

"The one through whom I will do this has not yet been born. He will be the son of your grandson Lamech – and so the ancestral line that will one day lead to the birth of the Savior will be preserved. That which I have promised will be accomplished.

"Enoch, I will also keep my promise regarding Methuselah and Lamech. They will not experience that day of judgment. I will permit them to die peacefully before that day arrives. Just as I promised you and Dayana, Methuselah's death will usher in the flood waters.

"And Enoch, you will not experience those days either – because I have a different assignment for you!"

But He did not tell me what the assignment was.

~

23

AND THEN . . . HE TOOK ME

~

That brings me back to where I began telling you my story. Another year has passed. Today God led me to a distant place. He placed my feet on a hill that overlooked a city. But this city is unlike any other I have ever seen. He told me we were standing there on a future day, and the name of the city is Jerusalem.

He told me His Promised One had already come. But instead of being welcomed and embraced, He was despised and rejected. Most people had turned their backs on Him and looked the other way.

I cried out, "Lord, they sound just like the people of my day – rejecting You – and rejecting Your truth!"

"Yes, they too have been deceived by the evil one," He continued. "Not only did they reject Him, but they also crucified Him on a cross on this very hill."

His voice momentarily faltered as He continued. "They spat on Him, they persecuted Him, and they murdered Him as if He were a common criminal. But what they did not realize was that through His death on that cross, He took upon Himself the sins of them all. He offered Himself as a sinless and spotless sacrifice so that their sins – and your sins, Enoch – could be forgiven.

"But He did not remain in the grave. On the third day, He arose – conquering sin and death! My Son became the second Adam. Physical life was given through your ancestor, the first Adam. But eternal life – life freed from the bondage of sin – was given through My Son, the second Adam. The work of redemption is complete. All who have turned to Him by faith will live with Me forever.

"My final judgment is at hand. This judgment will not be a flood. It is the judgment that you have foretold through the words I have given you! And My Son, the second Adam, the One whom they crucified, will soon return as King and Judge over all. As we look down upon this city, His return is but moments away.

"But, in My mercy and grace, I extended one last invitation to the people to repent of their sins and turn by faith to My Son. I sent two prophets to be olive trees and lampstands to stand among them declaring the day of salvation and judgment. They remained on the earth bearing witness for 1,260 days – but then the evil one and all those who follow him put them to death.

"They celebrated what they perceived to be their victory – just as they celebrated the death of My Son. But just like My Son, after three-and-one-half days, the spirit of life returned to them![1] All this occurred in the city below. I have brought you here to see where those final days took place!"

"Lord, who are the two witnesses who were killed?" I asked.

"They are two prophets I selected even before I created the earth. They are men who have been My faithful witnesses, whom I created and redeemed for just this purpose. They are men who lived on this earth in a prior day as prophets of old. They are men who faithfully completed the assignments I gave them in their day. And they are men I took from this earth without their having to experience death.

"They did not experience death then, because they experienced death in this future time. Because *it is appointed for men to die once, and after that comes the judgment.*[2] And once the spirit of life returned to the two witnesses, I shouted from heaven, *'Come up here!'* And they rose to heaven in a cloud as their enemies watched!"[3]

For a moment, He paused and we stood in silence. I had come to recognize over the years that God not only entrusts us with His Word, He also entrusts us with His silence. I learned to resist the temptation to run ahead and try to fill the silence with my words or actions. Rather, He taught me to be still, and know that He is God. In His perfect timing, He will break the silence. And in His time, He did.

"Enoch," He said, "you are one of those witnesses. I created you, chose you, and empowered you for this assignment. Just as My Spirit has gone with you throughout your past days, I will go with you in the days yet to come. You completed all I planned for you to do in these past days. Now it is time for you to come with Me and prepare for the remainder of My assignment for you.

"Today you began the day in your home here on earth, but you will end it with Me in your new home in heaven."

I hesitated for a moment because I had one question for my Lord. But He who knows our every thought already knew what was on my mind.

"No," He said, "you cannot return to your home to say goodbye to your family. I know that is hard. That is why I allowed Dayana to die early, so she would not be left to continue on by herself. Your sons will continue in the paths I have set before them. And one day soon, you will be reunited with them all."

"Lord, what will they think has happened to me?" I asked. "Will they think I have been eaten by a wild animal, or killed and buried like Cain did to Abel?"

"No," my Lord replied, "they will know that you faithfully walked with Me, and on this day, I took you. I will give their spirits that assurance. I will remind them and all generations that follow, that you pleased Me – and that it is impossible to please Me without faith!"[4]

I looked down at the city of Jerusalem one more time before I turned my gaze back on my Lord. In the twinkling of an eye, I was no more . . . because my Creator took me! And, oh, what a sight I now behold!

～

PLEASE HELP ME BY LEAVING A REVIEW!

i would be very grateful if you would leave a review of this book. Your feedback will be helpful to me in my future writing endeavors and will also assist others as they consider picking up a copy of the book.

To leave a review:

Go to: amazon.com/dp/1956866086

Or scan this QR code using your camera on your smartphone:

Thanks for your help!

∼

YOU WILL WANT TO READ ALL THE BOOKS IN "THE CALLED" SERIES

Stories of these ordinary men and women called by God to be used in extraordinary ways.

A Carpenter Called Joseph (Book 1)

A Prophet Called Isaiah (Book 2)

A Teacher Called Nicodemus (Book 3)

A Judge Called Deborah (Book 4)

A Merchant Called Lydia (Book 5)

A Friend Called Enoch (Book 6)

A Fisherman Called Simon (Book 7)

A Heroine Called Rahab (Book 8)

A Witness Called Mary (Book 9)

A Cupbearer Called Nehemiah (Book 10)

A Follower Called Mark (Book 11)

A Psalmist Called Asaph (Book 12) - Coming soon

AVAILABLE IN PAPERBACK, LARGE PRINT, AND FOR KINDLE ON AMAZON.

ALSO, A DISCUSSION GUIDE IS AVAILABLE AS A RESOURCE FOR YOUR SMALL GROUP OR BOOK CLUB AS YOU DISCUSS EACH OF THE BOOKS. AVAILABLE ON AMAZON IN PRINT OR FOR YOUR KINDLE.

Scan this QR code using your camera on your smartphone to see the entire series.

"THE PARABLES" SERIES

An Elusive Pursuit (Book 1)

Twenty-three year old Eugene Fearsithe boarded a train on the first day of April 1912 in pursuit of his elusive dream. Little did he know where the journey would take him, or what . . . and who . . . he would discover along the way.

Available on Amazon

A Belated Discovery (Book 2)

Nineteen year old Bobby Fearsithe enlisted in the army on the fifteenth day of December 1941 to fight for his family, his friends, and his neighbors. Along the way, he discovered just who his neighbor truly was.

Available on Amazon

Available in Hardcover, paperback, large print, audio, and for Kindle on Amazon.

Scan this QR code using your camera on your smartphone to see the entire series.

For more information, go to *kenwinter.org* or *wildernesslessons.com*

ALSO BY KENNETH A. WINTER

THROUGH THE EYES

(a series of biblical fiction novels)

Through the Eyes of a Shepherd (Shimon, a Bethlehem shepherd)

Through the Eyes of a Spy (Caleb, the Israelite spy)

Through the Eyes of a Prisoner (Paul, the apostle)

∾

THE EYEWITNESSES

(a series of biblical fiction short story collections)

For Christmas/Advent

Little Did We Know – the advent of Jesus — for adults

Not Too Little To Know – the advent – ages 8 thru adult

For Easter/Lent

The One Who Stood Before Us – the ministry and passion of Jesus — for adults

The Little Ones Who Came – the ministry and passion – ages 8 thru adult

∾

LESSONS LEARNED IN THE WILDERNESS SERIES

(a non-fiction series of biblical devotional studies)

The Journey Begins (Exodus) – Book 1

The Wandering Years (Numbers and Deuteronomy) – Book 2

Possessing The Promise (Joshua and Judges) – Book 3

Walking With The Master (The Gospels leading up to Palm Sunday) – Book 4

Taking Up The Cross (The Gospels – the passion through ascension) – Book 5

Until He Returns (The Book of Acts) – Book 6

ALSO AVAILABLE AS AUDIOBOOKS

THE CALLED series

A Carpenter Called Joseph

A Prophet Called Isaiah

A Teacher Called Nicodemus

A Judge Called Deborah

A Merchant Called Lydia

A Friend Called Enoch

A Fisherman Called Simon

A Heroine Called Rahab

A Witness Called Mary

A Cupbearer Called Nehemiah

A Follower Called Mark

✑

THROUGH THE EYES series

Through the Eyes of a Shepherd

Through the Eyes of a Spy

Through the Eyes of a Prisoner

✑

Little Did We Know

Not Too Little to Know

✑

THE PARABLES series

An Elusive Pursuit

A Belated Discovery

✑

SCRIPTURE BIBLIOGRAPHY

~

Much of the story line of this book is taken from the first six chapters of the Book of Genesis as recorded in Scripture. As explained in the preface, i also make references to The Book of Enoch, an apocryphal book.

Certain fictional events or depictions of those events have been added.

Some of the dialogue in this story are direct quotations from Scripture. Here are the specific references for those quotations:

Preface

[1] Genesis 5:21-22

[2] Jude 14

[3] Genesis 5:23

[4] 2 Kings 2:11

[5] Hebrews 9:27 (NASB)

[6] *The Book of Enoch*

[7] Jude 14-15

Chapter 1

[1] Adapted from Chapter 1 of *The Book of Enoch*

Chapter 2

[1] Genesis 1:28 (ESV)

[2] Genesis 3:17b-19a

Chapter 3

[1] Genesis 2:16-17

[2] Genesis 2:18

[3] Genesis 2:23

[4] Genesis 1:28-30

Chapter 4

[1] Genesis 3:1

[2] Genesis 3:2-3

[3] Genesis 3:4-5

[4] Genesis 3:9

[5] Genesis 3:10

[6] Genesis 3:11

[7] Genesis 3:12

[8] Genesis 3:13

[9] Genesis 3:13

Chapter 5

[1] Genesis 3:14-15

(2) Genesis 3:16

(3) Genesis 3:17-19

(4) Genesis 3:22

Chapter 6

(1) Genesis 4:1

Chapter 8

(1) Genesis 4:6-7

Chapter 9

(1) Genesis 4:9

(2) Genesis 4:9

(3) Genesis 4:10-12

(4) Genesis 4:13-14

(5) Genesis 4:15

(6) Genesis 4:24

Chapter 10

(1) Genesis 4:25

(2) Genesis 3:15

Chapter 17

(1) Ezekiel 28:12 (ESV)

Chapter 18

(1) Adapted from Section 1, Chapter 6 of *The Book of Enoch*

(2) Genesis 6:7

Chapter 19

(1) Genesis 6:3

Chapter 20

(1) Adapted from Section 2, Chapters 37, 41, 46, 47, 48, 51, 54 of *The Book of Enoch*

(2) Jude 14-15

Chapter 21

(1) Adapted from Section 3, Chapter 82 of *The Book of Enoch*

(2) Adapted from Section 5, Chapter 91 of *The Book of Enoch*

Chapter 22

(1) Adapted from Genesis 6:17-21 (spoken by God to Noah, not Enoch)

Chapter 23

(1) Revelation 11:3-11

(2) Hebrews 9:27 (NASB)

(3) Revelation 11:12

(4) Hebrews 11:5-6

References to *The Book of Enoch* are taken from *The Book of Enoch*, The Apocrypha and Pseudepigrapha of the Old Testament, edited by H. R. Charles Oxford, published by The Clarendon Press

≈

LISTING OF CHARACTERS
(ALPHABETICAL ORDER)

~

Many of the characters in this book are real people pulled directly from the pages of Scripture. i have not changed any details about a number of those individuals, except the addition of their interactions with the fictional characters. They are noted below as "UN" (unchanged).

In other instances, fictional details have been added to real people to provide backgrounds about their lives where Scripture is silent. The intent is that you understand these were real people, whose lives were full of the many details that fill our own lives. They are noted as "FB" (fictional background).

In some instances, we are never told the names of certain individuals in the Bible. In those instances, where i have given them a name as well as a fictional background, they are noted as "FN" (fictional name).

Lastly, a number of the characters are purely fictional, added to convey the fictional elements of these stories. They are noted as "FC" (fictional character).

∽

Abel – second son of Adam & Eve (FB)

Adah – wife of Lamech (line of Cain), mother of Jabal & Jubal (UN)

Adam/ Abot – the first man, created by God, father of Cain, Awan, Abel & Seth (FB)

Aviv – eldest son of Enoch & Dayana (FC)

Awan – eldest daughter of Adam & Eve, wife of Cain (FC)

Cain – eldest son of Adam & Eve, husband of Awan (FB)

Chava – wife of Seth, mother of Enosh

Dayana – wife of Enoch, mother of Aviv & Methuselah (FC)

Enoch, son of Cain – eldest son of Cain & Awan (UN)

Enoch, son of Jared – son of Jared, husband of Dayana, father of Aviv & Methuselah, prophet of God (FB)

Enosh – son of Seth & Chava, father of Kenan (FB)

Eve/ Matre – the first woman, created by God, wife of Adam, mother of Cain, Awan, Abel & Seth (FB)

Jabal – son of Lamech & Adah (line of Cain) (UN)

Jared – son of Mahalalel, father of Enoch & Shep (FB)

Jobab – leader of fictional village of Larak (FC)

Jubal – son of Lamech & Adah (line of Cain) (UN)

Kenan – son of Enosh, father of Mahalalel (FB)

Lamech, son of Methuselah – son of Methuselah, husband of Shira, father of Noah (FB)

Lamech, son of Methushael – great-great-great-grandson of Cain & Awan (FB)

Mahalalel – son of Kenan, father of Jared (FB)

Methuselah – son of Enoch, husband of Mira, father of Lamech (FB)

Mira – wife of Methuselah, mother of Lamech (FC)

Obal – great-grandson of Tubal-cain (FC)

Semjaza – leader of fallen angels (named in the Book of Enoch) (FC)

Seth – son of Adam & Eve, inherited birthright, husband of Chava, father of Enosh (FB)

Shep – son of Jared, younger brother of Enoch (FC)

Shira – wife of Lamech, mother of Noah (FC)

The Creator – the Sovereign and Almighty God (UN)

The Promised One – Jesus Christ, the Son of God (UN)

Tubal-cain – son of Lamech & Zillah (the line of Cain) (UN)

Unnamed wife of Enosh – mother of Kenan (UN)

Unnamed wife of Jared – mother of Enoch & Shep (FC)

Zillah – second wife of Lamech (the line of Cain), mother of Tubal-cain (UN)

∼

ACKNOWLEDGMENTS

I do not cease to give thanks for you ….
Ephesians 1:16 (ESV)

… my partner in all things, LaVonne,
for choosing to trust God as we walk with Him in this faith adventure;

… my family,
for your love, support and encouragement always;

… Sheryl,
for enabling me to tell the story in a far better way;

… Scott,
for your artistry and creativity;

… a precious group of friends
(many of whom have stuck with me through all of my books)
who have read an advance copy of this book,
for all of your help, feedback and encouragement;

… and most importantly,
the One who is truly the Author and Finisher of it all
– our Lord and Savior Jesus Christ!

∽

ABOUT THE AUTHOR

 Ken Winter is a follower of Jesus, an extremely blessed husband, and a proud father and grandfather – all by the grace of God. His journey with Jesus has led him to serve on the pastoral staffs of two local churches – one in West Palm Beach, Florida and the other in Richmond, Virginia – and as the vice president of mobilization of the IMB, an international missions organization.

Today, Ken continues in that journey as a full-time author, teacher and speaker. You can read his weekly blog posts at kenwinter.blog and listen to his weekly podcast at kenwinter.org/podcast.

And we proclaim Him, admonishing every man and teaching every man with all wisdom, that we may present every man complete in Christ. And for this purpose also I labor, striving according to His power, which mightily works within me.
(Colossians 1:28-29 NASB)

PLEASE JOIN MY READERS' GROUP

Please join my Readers' Group in order to receive updates and information about future releases, etc.

Also, i will send you a free copy of *The Journey Begins* e-book — the first book in the *Lessons Learned In The Wilderness* series. It is yours to keep or share with a friend or family member that you think might benefit from it.

It's completely free to sign up. i value your privacy and will not spam you. Also, you can unsubscribe at any time.

Go to kenwinter.org to subscribe.

Or scan this QR code using your camera on your smartphone:

∽

35397083R00073